It Was Only One Damn Night 3

A novel by Lady Lissa

Previously in book two...

Marcus

Kalisha didn't give up. For the past two days she had been calling my job like she was my side chick. The shit was embarrassing to be getting all these pink messages from Lynette's nosey ass. I couldn't understand what was so important that she had to keep calling me. I was sure by now she had the test results and the kid wasn't mine. I told her when those results came back, I was done with her. But she was seriously tripping on me right now.

I had Lynette lie and tell her that I was in a meeting every single time she called. I prayed she would get the message and stop calling me. Like damn, didn't she get the picture that I didn't want to be bothered? What kind of question was that? Of course, she didn't.

I gave her 20 G's and she was still bothering the fuck out of me. If someone had given me that much money, I would forget why the fuck I was trying to get in touch with them. I would just let the shit be, but I could tell Kalisha wasn't about to do that.

However, had I just answered her call, none of the events that followed would've ever happened. I was sitting at my desk busting my ass when my wife came busting into my office. The look on her face had me thinking some crazy shit. What was wrong with her? Where were the girls? Did someone die?

"Babe what are you doing here? Where are the twins?" I asked nervously.

She was breathing hot and heavy like she was having a heart attack or something. "What's wrong with you? Did something happen to my mom? Did something happen to Ms. Belinda?" I continued questioning her. I was now standing in her face trying to figure out what was wrong with my wife, but she wasn't telling me shit.

"Why did you come here baby? What is the problem?"

She dug in her purse and pulled out an envelope. She handed it to me. Shit, it looked like the average letter addressed to me in a woman's handwriting.

Oh Lord, she thinks I'm cheating.

That was the first thought that popped into my head.

"What the fuck is this?" I asked.

"Open it," she said. She stood there with her arms over her chest.

I opened the envelope and pulled out the letter. I started reading it and my mouth fell to the floor. I looked up at my wife who had tears in her eyes. But as hurt as she was, she still managed to punch the shit out of me.

POW!

Chapter one

Melina

Marcus had gone back to work about two weeks ago, and I'd be lying if I said I didn't miss my man. I missed him helping me with the kids, but I understood that he had to get back to work. Thank God my mom was here helping me out because I didn't know what I'd do without her. Even though I missed Marcus, I was kind of glad he went back to work.

As much as I loved him, he was irking my last nerve. I kept trying to get him to take that paternity test, but he kept claiming that he was too busy. I was thinking that it might be a good idea to invite Kalisha somewhere private so we could get the test done.

I was starting to think that we may have to meet up at Marcus' office. I bought a home test kit from Walgreens but hadn't told Marcus about it. I was going to reach out to Kalisha and ask if she could meet me at his office next week to surprise him. I figured if we both showed up with the baby, he wouldn't have a choice but to take that damn test.

I was just tired of the uncertainty, ya know? I needed answers and I needed them now. My husband wouldn't be avoiding this woman the way that he was if he didn't have anything to worry about. He was running and hiding from her because something happened between them. I wished I could prove it without the DNA test, but I couldn't. I thought about reaching out to his brother Kendrick and asking him about that night but decided against it.

I just didn't want to put anyone else in our business. Besides, there was no guarantee that Kendrick would tell me the truth. Come to find out, I didn't even have to go through all that to find out what the truth was. The truth showed up on my fucking doorstep.

"Mom I'm going check the mail!" I called out.

She was sitting in the living room watching *The Bold & The Beautiful.* I didn't understand how she could watch that soap opera. Those rich white people seemed to have more drama and lies than poor black people. I walked outside to the mailbox and started going through the mail as I walked back towards the front door. When I saw a letter addressed to Marcus, I wondered who it was from. There was no return address, but the handwriting definitely belonged to a woman.

I knew it was illegal to open someone else's mail, but I didn't think the courts would mind since me and my husband shared the same address. What I read made me plop down on a chair in the kitchen nook. It was a letter from Kalisha informing Marcus that he was indeed the father of her little boy. The letter went like this...

Hey Marcus, I tried to reach you at your job, but the receptionist keeps saying that you're in a meeting. I know you weren't in a meeting every time I called, so since you're back to avoiding me again, Anyway, I received the results of the DNA test, which was why I was trying to reach you. Since you wanna play games, I decided to send the test results to your house. I tried to be adult about this, but you keep playing games. I'm not going to keep chasing you to be a part of OUR son's life! I shouldn't have to do that. If you can spend time with your daughters, you should be able to spend time with your son.

I'm not even trying to be a bitch about it. I'd like to get to know your wife and maybe we could be cordial with each other for the sake of the kids. However, since neither of you want anything to do with me and you want nothing to do with your son, I guess that's something I'll have to live with. Just forward the checks to the address on the letter.

P.S. I got your address from the checks you gave me. Thanks a lot because that money will definitely come in handy.

Your baby mama, Kalisha

When I read OUR SON in all caps, I started breathing hard and having chest pains. By the time I got to the end of the letter with the discussion of money, I was livid. I looked at the other paper that was inside the envelope with the letter and it was the test results for a DNA test I didn't know had been taken. That nigga had told me he was too busy to take those tests, so how the hell did he end up taking them with her.

I had asked Marcus about that woman and if he slept with her and he told me no. He constantly told me no. I asked him was he sure and if there was a possibility that her baby boy was his. He still said no. But he had lied to me.

I grabbed my purse, stuffed the envelope in it then went to ask my mom to watch the girls. "Mom there's something I need to handle right now. Can you watch the girls?"

"What's wrong?" she asked. She immediately turned her TV off and came over to me.

"Nothing mom, I'm fine."

"No, you're not fine. You don't think I know my child? I'm your mother. That means I know you better than anyone, including yourself. What's wrong?" she asked again.

"I can't talk about this right now. Can you just watch the girls for me please?"

"Yes, of course," she said.

"Thanks. I'll be back soon."

I rushed out the door and hopped in my Cadillac Escalade, a push gift from my husband. I wondered if he bought that truck for me out of guilt. I hoped that wasn't the reason because it wasn't going back. I deserved this truck for pushing out the twins, so that was that. As I started down the highway, the thought of Marcus sleeping with Kalisha angered me. But you know what else I felt... pain.

My heart was literally breaking at the thought of my husband being unfaithful to me. Then he had the nerve to have unprotected sex with her. What if she would've had an STD? He could've brought that shit back to me.

I didn't even realize I was crying until my tears slid into my lap. We had been in counseling for over a year. I had given him ample opportunities to tell me the truth, but he still chose to lie. If he had told me the truth, we might have been able to work things out. After all, according to the two of them, it was only one night. It wasn't as if they had an ongoing affair.

Had my husband told me the truth, we could have spoken to our therapist about it and gotten past it. I was sure of that because I loved my husband, and the family that we now had. He had tossed all that shit out the window the minute he decided to lie to me. As I pulled into the parking lot of his job, I tried to calm myself down so I wouldn't make a scene in front of the people in the lobby. However, I couldn't smile to save my fucking life right now.

Before I got out of the truck, I reread the letter just to make sure that I was giving him facts. Kalisha mentioned something about getting our address off a check Marcus had given her. I hadn't been paying too much attention to our bank account because I had no reason to worry. Marcus and I had done a good job stacking up our paper in both the checking and savings accounts.

But if he had taken money from any of those accounts to pay Kalisha, we had a huge problem. I logged into the banking app on my phone and checked the transactions. It didn't seem like anything out of the ordinary. So, what check was she talking about? It seemed that my husband had way too many fucking secrets these days, but it was time for me to get to the bottom of it.

I took a deep breath and got out of the truck. Securing the lock, I smoothed my dress and walked into the building. I hit the up button and when the elevator came, I pressed the button to Marcus' floor. My hands shook as the elevator climbed to the third floor. When it finally dinged, I couldn't get off that bitch fast enough.

I walked up to the receptionist desk and was greeted by Sasha.

"Hello Mrs. O'Connor, congratulations on the twins! I saw pictures on Mr. O'Connor's desk. They're beautiful!" she gushed with a huge smile on her face.

"Thank you, Sasha. Is Marcus in his office?"

"Yes, would you like me to tell him you're here?"

"No, I'll be fine. Please hold his calls for the next half hour," I said.

"Half hour?"

"Thank you, Sasha," I said with a stern look on my face as I walked away.

I busted in Marcus' office and I knew he thought the Terminator was coming to exterminate his ass. The look on his face was one of confusion, fright, and worry all mixed into one.

Babe what are you doing here? Where are the twins?" he asked

What kind of fucking question was that? Where are the twins? Where the hell did he think they were? My mom had been staying with us for the past two and a half weeks. As I thought about his bullshit question, I started getting mad all over again. I mean, really mad!

"What's wrong with you? Did something happen to my mom? Did something happen to Ms. Belinda?" He was asking so many questions, but I could tell that he was nervous.

He didn't need to be nervous, but he should be very afraid because with the way I was feeling right now, I didn't know what I was capable of. I couldn't even respond to his freaking questions because I was so pissed.

"Why did you come here baby? What is the problem?"

I stuck my trembling hand in my purse and pulled out the envelope. I thrust it at him and shoved it in his hand. He looked at it like it was a death sentence. Shit, it just might be one. As he continued to look at the envelope, I was wondering what was taking him so long to open it.

Lord, let me find out that he already knew what was in the envelope. I swear if he already knows, he will be coming to see you tonight.

"What the fuck is this?" he asked.

"Open it," I said as I stood there waiting for him to finish reading the letter.

As he read the first page, I could see the shock in his eyes. Then he looked at the other page that held the DNA results before staring at me with his mouth hung wide open. Before he could say anything, I punched him dead in his lying ass mouth. I wasn't about to let him open his mouth and tell me another lie. I needed everyone to know that I wasn't a violent person by any means, and that was the first time I had ever put my hands- on Marcus in that manner. I was actually scared of myself for a minute.

Scared that I was actually capable of this kind of violence. However, as shocked by my actions as I was, there was no way in hell I was about to apologize for what I had done. My husband was old enough to know that for every action there was a reaction. So, the last thing I was going to do was tell my husband that I was sorry. Why not? Because I would have been lying. In that moment, I felt absolutely justified for my reaction.

"Okay, I had that coming," he said.

"You got a lot more than that coming! What the fuck Marcus?! You said you never slept with her even though I asked you time and time again! I begged you to tell me the truth, but instead of being honest with me, you continued to lie to me!" I wailed as he stood there holding his mouth.

I didn't think I had hit him that hard, but I guess I didn't know my own strength. I had busted his bottom lip but thank God it wasn't that bad.

"Babe I..."

"Uh uh, don't say shit to me! Ever since we ran into that woman the first time when she claimed that you were her baby's father, I asked you. I asked you that day and kept asking you weeks and months later. That's how long you had to tell me the truth... months! When I first saw that little boy, in the back of my mind, I knew he was yours. He looks just like yo ass!" I said as I threw my hands up. When I tell you that nigga flinched hard, his eyes closed for a brief minute. "But when I asked you if that was your son, you swore you never slept with that girl! I believed you... even though in my gut I knew you were lying!" That was when the tears started.

"Babe, I wanted to tell you..."

"You wanted to tell me what Marcus? What? That you had a son outside of our marriage! Huh?!"

"No, I really didn't think her son was mine..."

"YOUR SON!! He is your son!!"

"I know that now, but I didn't believe it then..."

"I don't see how! He looks just like you and the girls!"

"I wanted to tell you about that night, but..."

"But what Marcus? I gave you ample opportunity to tell me. Why didn't you?" I asked as the tears continued to spill.

"I didn't know how."

"You didn't know how? Even though we were in counseling and talking about our issues? You didn't know how?"

'Babe that was something I had never come to you about. I didn't know how to tell you no shit like that!"

"Marcus you could've been honest about that one night. You and Kalisha said it was JUST ONE NIGHT!!" I said as I held my forefinger in his face.

"Yea, that's all it was babe! JUST ONE FUCKIN' NIGHT! I swear!" he said.

"You don't have to swear Marcus, I believe you when you said it was one- night. If you had told me that when I asked you the first time, we wouldn't be discussing it now!" I said. "When we ran into that girl at the doctor's office that first time, I asked you to be honest with me! We're going to a counselor for a reason! We were going to save our marriage, and what's the one thing the therapist always said we need in our marriage!"

"Trust," he said with a sad expression on his face.

"Exactly! How the hell am I supposed to trust you after this Marcus?" I asked. "All you had to do was tell me the truth! That's all I asked!"

"I know babe, and I'm so sorry that I didn't tell the truth," he said as he reached for me.

"Don't you dare put your fucking hands on me!" I snarled as I smacked him upside the head. "You did a DNA test with her behind my back! I had been asking you when you wanted to go. I kept telling you Marcus we need to go get that test done, so we can get this girl off your back! You kept telling me that you were so busy at the office and you didn't have the time! But it's funny how you made time for Kalisha..."

"Babe that's not true!"

"THAT IS TRUE!"

"Babe I swear to you, she just showed up here uninvited and unannounced after she looked me up on Google! I guess she got my last name from the doctor's office! I swear I didn't wanna take that damn test! But I took it because I just wanted to get her out of my damn life... out of our lives! I had hoped the test would be negative and she would leave me the hell alone!"

"And look how that turned out! You came home and never told me anything about that meeting or that you had taken the test!" I said. "Did you sleep with her again?"

"What? Aw, HELL NAW!!"

"Then I don't know why you would hide something so important from me! I AM YOUR WIFE MARCUS!! YOUR WIFE!!"

"I know, and I'm so sorry..."

"Well, let's talk about the money you gave her! What money Marcus? Where did you get the money? Because our account isn't short. Where did you get money to give that girl and how much did you give her?"

"Babe can we finish this conversation when I get home?" he asked as he checked his watch for the time. "I have a meeting in about 20 minutes, and I need to prepare for it."

"Oh, sure. We can talk about it at home. Then you can pack your shit and get the fuck out of my house!"

"What?" The look he gave me held so much hurt that I heard it in his voice.

"I can't do this with you Marcus. You deliberately lied to my face on more than one occasion. We've been in counseling, so you know how important it is to be honest in our marriage, but you didn't do that." Tears began to stream down my face, so I reached for a tissue on his desk. There was no way I was going to walk out of this office looking anything different than when I came in.

"Melina please, babe..."

I held my hand up to get him to stop talking, but it took me a minute to get my words out. I was crying so hard that I was choked up.

"You don't have to say anything Marcus. Just know that you hurt me. My entire soul has been crushed by the one person who was supposed to protect me. Oh God!" I cried as I gulped in sorrow. The fierce amount of pain I was feeling was overwhelming. I had to get the hell up out of here.

I dried my eyes as best I could and walked out of the office. No one needed to know what I had just gone down in my husband's office. I had managed to hold my head high until I got back in my truck. Once inside the truck, I released all the pain I had been forced to keep bottled up inside me while I rode the elevator and walked through the lobby of the first floor.

I cried harder than I had ever cried in my entire life. My marriage was over... no ifs, ands, or buts about it.

Chapter two

Kalisha

I felt pretty good these days. I had finally received the news that I had been waiting for. Marcus could no longer deny that my son was also his. I had just put my baby down for a nap and was sitting on the sofa with my laptop computer browsing through the apartment listings.

"Maybe I should get a house," I said out loud.

I knew a house would be bigger, but at least my baby would have a backyard. I'd be able to put in a swing set and he and I could play ball. Living in an apartment wouldn't allow us the privacy that my baby deserved. With the money that Marcus gave me, of course, I couldn't afford to buy a house, but I could rent a nice one. I would probably consider buying a house one day. Hell, I'd definitely be able to afford it now that my baby daddy was rich.

KNOCK! KNOCK! KNOCK!

"Who the hell is that?"

I placed my laptop on the sofa and stood up. I went to the door and opened it to find Marcus' wife standing there. "I'm sorry for just showing up at your place, but we need to talk," she said as she walked into my apartment.

"Well damn! Come on in," I said sarcastically.

"Look Kalisha, I don't know what kind of game you're playing..."

"Hold up! What makes you think I'm playing a game?" I asked.

"Because you sent the test results to my house!"

"Okay, maybe I didn't go about that the right way, but what did you expect me to do when Marcus wasn't taking any of my calls?" I asked. "I mean, even you said you were gonna call me, but did you? No!"

"I would have called you had Marcus been not so busy with work."

"Well, that's why I took matters into my own hands."

"Marcus said you showed up at his office one night with the test," she said.

"That's right! I was tired waiting for y'all to call me!"

"So, what money did Marcus give you?"

"Shouldn't you be discussing this with your husband?" I asked.

"I'm asking you, woman to woman. How much money did Marcus give you?" she repeated.

"He gave me enough…"

"Enough for what?"

Well damn! Obviously, her and Marcus were having some issues. I wasn't sure why his wife was even here right now. "Enough to take care of our kid. What is this about? Didn't your husband talk to you about this before he did it?"

The look on her face when I asked the question told me everything I needed to know. Marcus hadn't spoken to her about the money he had given me. I just didn't know why she wasn't firing her questions at him instead of me. We didn't even know each other like that for her to come to my apartment. Speaking of which…

"How did you figure out where I lived?"

"From the letter you sent to my house! Now that you have your test results proving that Marcus is your son's father, what are you going to do with that?" Melina asked.

"What's that supposed to mean?"

"I mean, you were adamant that he was the father…"

"Which he is!"

"Right, but what do you think is going to happen now that you've proven your point," she asked.

"Well, to be honest, I haven't thought that far ahead yet. But all I really wanted was for Marcus to step up and be a father to my son. I want him to come by and visit..."

"Not gonna happen!"

"What? Are you really going to be a petty Betty and keep Marcus from spending time with his firstborn, with his only son?"

Wouldn't that be about a bitch for her to stop her husband from accepting responsibility for our son? What kind of mother would keep a baby from his father?

"Oh, I'm not gonna stop him from spending time with his son, but he won't be doing it here with you!" she said.

"Oh, so you're intimidated by me..." I said as I clicked my tongue in my mouth.

"Girl bye! Look at you and look at me! Is that vomit on your shirt?" she asked as she made a stank face.

I had forgotten that Cameron had spit up on my shirt earlier. This woman was really feeling herself right now. Acting like she was better than me. What the hell made her better than me? Her man? Her clothes? Her expensive car? That didn't make her better than me. And the fact that she came over here right now showed me that she was worried about me in their lives.

"All I wanted was to tell Marcus something he needed to know," I said as I propped my right hand on my hip.

"And you thought sending the results to my house..."

"I'm sorry but I thought y'all were married and it was his house too," I said.

"His house, my house, the fact of the matter is you should have sent him an email or something!"

"So, wait a minute. Are you mad at me because I delivered the news or because your husband is my baby daddy?"

"I'm upset with you because of your deliverance! You keep talking about how you're this grown ass woman and shit, but that right there was some childish shit!" she said.

"Okay, well, maybe I could've delivered the news to his office, but he wouldn't answer his phone. I figured if he wasn't answering his phone, he sure wasn't going to see me if I went over to his office," I said. "As for sending him an email, I don't have it."

"That shit was childish and petty. You wanna know what I think?"

"Oh, do tell..."

"I think you want my husband..."

"How you figure that?" I asked.

"Let me tell you something lil girl..."

"Lil girl?"

"I'm just calling it as I see it. Marcus may be your baby's father, but he will never be with you. You wanna know why? Because you're immature and childish. I don't know what he saw in you that night y'all slept together. Oh yea, he was drunk. I don't know what your angle is, but it's not working. He will never want you!" Melina said as she turned on her heels and walked toward the front door.

"It's hard to believe that your man would be interested in a chick like me, huh? Just cuz I don't have that expensive weave down my back and those red bottoms, he couldn't possibly want me, huh? But guess what... he did!"

"He was drunk! Had he been in his right mind, he never would've stooped so low..."

"And yet he did! Whether he was drunk or not, he still chose a bitch like me," I said as I pointed to myself.

"Just stay the fuck away from my husband!"

"Oh, you mean my baby daddy?!"

"No, I mean MY HUSBAND!!" she said.

She looked me up and down and started laughing like something about me was funny. What the hell was so fucking funny? So, I had on ripped shorts and a camisole top instead of her designer duds and expensive shoes like she did. I was at home and dealing with a baby who spit on me at least three times a day. Without another word from either of us, she laughed her way out the door.

I wanted to run behind her and cuss her out but didn't want to feel stupid. I looked at my image in the mirror on the wall and almost threw up. No wonder she thought I was a joke. I looked like a damn joke with my hair all over the place and dried up baby vomit on my shirt.

"Ugh!" I cried as I threw my remote control against the wall.

That noise woke Cameron, so I went running to the nursery to get him. "Ssshhhh! It's okay mommy's baby. I gotchu," I shushed him as I picked him up.

I cradled him in my arms as I walked to the kitchen to fix my baby a bottle. I fed him as I rocked him in the rocker with the ottoman that I had recently purchased with the money Marcus gave me. I had told Donya that Marcus had only given me 10 G's because I didn't need her telling Joy or Porsha my business. Porsha relied on Chandler for support, but Joy was always looking for one of us to loan her money. She had a job at Walmart but could never make her ends meet.

If Joy knew that Marcus had given me any money, her hand would definitely be out. And considering the fact that I had a son to raise and a baby daddy who was shirking his responsibilities, I didn't have money to be giving away. Not only that, but I didn't need my mom finding out that I had gotten $20,000 from my baby daddy. She was always looking to take someone else's money to get rich at the casino.

I didn't talk about my mom much because she and I had fallen out over money several times. She liked to play the slot machines. That was one of the main reasons I barely reached out to her. She loved flying to Vegas or Atlantic City or driving to Louisiana just to play the slots. I couldn't have her spending my money on bullshit.

After I fed Cameron, I changed his diaper then put him in his swing in front of the television. I sat back on the sofa, grabbed my laptop and started my search for a new place to stay.

BOOM! BOOM! BOOM!

"Damn! Who the fuck banging on my door like the fuckin' po po?!"

I slid my laptop back on the sofa and went to the door. I pulled the door open and Marcus rushed inside my apartment. "What the fuck Kalisha?!" he fussed. "Why the fuck would you send this shit to my house yo?!" He was waving what I assumed were the test results and the letter I sent.

"Okay, calm down…"

"CALM DOWN?!! ARE YOU FUCKING SERIOUS RIGHT NOW?!!"

Damn, he was really mad! Shit, well, I was mad too, but didn't nobody care about that. Like, we had sex and he ghosted me for an entire nine months. Then when I finally got the information I needed to track him down, so we could get the damn test done, he started avoiding my calls.

"Well, what did you expect me to do? You weren't taking my calls at your job and I didn't have your cell…"

"I don't give a fuck! What the hell were you thinking sending this shit to my house?"

"I was thinking that I finally got the results and you needed to know that you have a son! Look, maybe sending the results to your house wasn't the best option, but it was the only option I had. I tried to reach you at work, but you wouldn't answer my calls or call me back! What did you expect me to do?" I asked as I folded my arms across my chest.

"That's a trick question, right?"

"No, it's a real one! You've been denying my son, OUR SON, this whole time and now that you have the results, you can't deny him anymore! Cameron is your son, your firstborn Marcus!"

"I didn't ask for this shit Kalisha!"

"And I did? I didn't know that you were married when I invited you in my home! Had I known that shit, I never would've come on to you that night!" I argued.

"Right! There it is!" he yelled as he clapped his hands. "You came on to me! I didn't want this shit!"

"I didn't think I was going to get pregnant that night Marcus! It wasn't as if I was looking for it either, but we have a son now!"

"Man, shit wasn't even supposed to be this way!" he said as he ran his hand down his face.

"Damn, things must really be bad on the home front, huh? First, I got a visit from your wife, and now you…"

"Wait! Melina was here?"

"Yea."

"When?"

"She just left a couple of hours ago. And I must say that I didn't appreciate her coming here to look down on me either!"

"Man, you done fucked up everything in my fucking life!"

"I FUCKED UP EVERYHTING IN YOUR LIFE MARCUS?!! WHAT ABOUT MY LIFE?!!"

"You're the one who wanted to fuck! YOU SAID IT YOURSELF, YOU CAME ON TO ME!!" he yelled, as he banged his fist on his chest causing Cameron to burst into tears.

I rushed over to him and scooped him up, trying to comfort him and get him to quiet down. "So, because I came on to you, I should have to raise our baby by myself?" I asked.

"I don't give a fuck who you raise him with! I don't want any parts..."

"Marcus, really? You're going to walk away from this precious little boy because of what? Because you're scared to lose your precious family?" I asked angrily. "Why can't you love our son the way you love those little girls? He didn't ask to be in this world! You helped me to bring him into this world, and we owe it to him to give him the best life possible!" I was crying at this point because my feelings were really hurt. How could he continue to deny our son after the test showed he was the father?

"Nah, you owe him that..."

"Look at this baby! Look at him!" I cried as I thrust my son in his face.

Cameron looked at Marcus while squirming in my arms. As the two locked eyes on each other, I saw something shift in Marcus' eyes. It was like he was seeing his son for the first time. He took the crying baby from me and held him. Tears streamed from his eyes as he held our little boy for the first time. I was crying too, but you know who wasn't crying? Cameron. As soon as Marcus took him from me, his crying stopped.

This was all I wanted... for Marcus to acknowledge my little boy as his just the way he did the girls. I could tell that things were finally going to be different now.

Chapter three

Marcus

The last thing I expected was for my wife to bust into my office with those paternity test results. I was hoping that the test would have turned out that I wasn't that little boy's daddy, then I could get on with my life. But when I saw the 99.99999% positive at the bottom of the page, all I could think of was how I fucked up. Then Kalisha had the nerve to mention the money I gave her fucking stupid ass! I should've never given her shit!

I just thought she'd take the money and get the fuck out of my life, but no. The bitch was making shit ten times worse. My wife and I had put that shit behind us, well somewhat anyway. As I looked up into my wife's tear- filled eyes, Melina didn't even give me a chance to say shit before she punched me in my damn mouth. I deserved that shit though. I should've never lied to my wife.

Melina and I had been through so much shit. I should've just been honest about my one- night with Kalisha. She said if I would've been honest, we could've worked it out. Now, I didn't know if that was possible. She didn't want shit to do with me. She even told me to pack my shit and get out. My nerves were on tens now because I didn't know how I was going to fix this mess Kalisha had made.

After my meeting was over, I couldn't get out of my office fast enough. I headed to Kalisha's house pissed to the fucking max. I couldn't believe she had been so inconsiderate and petty. That was definitely a petty fucking move she made sending that shit to my house like that. I think she wanted my wife to know about the test and results. I wondered if she would've sent those results to my house if the test would've been negative.

I had no idea when I got to her place that she would throw my son in my face. Yea, I said my son. Once I held the little boy in my arms, there was no denying that he was my kid. He looked just like me when I was a baby. His sisters resembled him too. They all had my nose and the little chinks around their eyes. Aw man, what the fuck had I done?

"I told you that he was yours. I never lied to you," Kalisha said as she stroked my arm.

I flinched back at her touch. "Don't do that!" I said.

"Sorry. I just got caught up in the moment," she said.

"Just make sure you don't get caught up in it again."

What Kalisha and I had was one night. One fucking night that I wished I could erase, but it was impossible at this point. I knew that my son didn't ask to be here, and it wasn't his fault. But with all the shit going on, I really didn't need this. However, I was going to do my best to take care of him. I owed him that.

I handed the baby back to Kalisha. "I gotta go!" I said.

"What? You're leaving already?"

"I gotta go home and try to do some damage control. You fucked up my entire marriage, so now I gotta make things right with my wife!"

"What about Cameron? What about making things right with him?" she asked.

"I just did! I acknowledged that he was my son, didn't I?" I asked.

What the fuck did this chick want from me? Because if it was anything more than a baby daddy, she had the wrong nigga!

"Wow! After chasing you for a year, you're just gonna up and leave him?"

"That little boy will still be here tomorrow and the day after. I gotta fix my marriage, girl!" I said as I turned towards the door.

"Then go! Don't worry about me trying to get in touch with you again! If you don't wanna be in our son's life, fuck it!" she said angrily.

I turned around and looked at her. "You know what? I'm starting to think that you're looking for me to be more than your baby's daddy."

"Boy please!" she scoffed. "All I ever wanted was for you to accept Cameron as your son!"

"And I've done that! But because of the shit that you pulled by sending those results to my crib, now I got some work to do with my wife!"

"Is she more important than your son!"

"SHE'S MORE IMPORTANT THAN YOU!!" I yelled.

I opened the door and slammed it shut behind me. Kalisha was up to some scandalous shit, and I didn't want to be a part of that. As soon as I got in the truck, I called our therapist.

"Good afternoon, Dr. Bryant's office. How may I help you?" greeted Ashley, the receptionist.

"This is Marcus O'Connor. I have an emergency and need to speak to Dr. Bryant," I said.

"Let me see if she's available." She clicked the line over then clicked it back.

"This is Dr. Bryant."

"Dr. Bryant, this is Marcus. I need your help," I said.

"What's going on?"

"Can you meet me at my house? I'm on my way there now, and my wife is threatening to throw me out!"

"Oh my! What in the world?"

"It's a long story and I promise to explain everything as soon as I see you, but I really need you to meet me at my house ASAP!" I stated.

"Okay, I'm on my way," she said.

"Thank you so much!"

I ended the call and continued driving to my house. I prayed that Melina hadn't discussed any of this with her mom because me and Ms. Belinda and I got along pretty well. This news here would definitely tear the relationship I had with my mother in law apart. All I could think about on the drive home was that I should've been honest with my wife. I hit the steering wheel again.

"Please say your command!"

"Call mom!" I said.

"Calling mom!"

"Hey baby..."

"Mom I need you to come to the house as soon as possible," I said.

"Marcus? What's going on baby?" my mom asked nervously. I didn't want to worry her, but I knew if I was going to get my wife to listen to me, I needed to have my mom present.

"Mom it's a long story, but I did something really stupid and Melina is pissed at me. I need you to come to the house and help Ms. Belinda take care of the twins while me and Melina talk," I said.

"What did you do honey?"

"I'll explain everything to you later mom. Can you please come to the house?"

"Yea, just let me grab my purse and I'll be on my way."

"Thanks mom," I said.

"You're welcome baby. I don't know what you did but pray on it, baby. God will get you through this," she said. That was my mom's answer to everything... pray on it.

I would pray on it, but I didn't think God would be able to get me out of this shit.

"I am mom. Thanks."

"See you soon."

Our call ended and 15 minutes later, I pulled into my driveway. I hopped out of the truck as soon as I had shifted the gear to park. I rushed in the house and went in search of my wife. I found her in the nursery rocking Marina while her mom rocked Karina. Melina looked at me with tears threatening to fall as she rolled her eyes.

"I'm not sure what's going on between you two, but I hope that you can fix it for your girls. I know that the two of you love each other, so Marcus," Ms. Belinda said as she turned her attention to me. "I pray that whatever you did doesn't cost you your family."

I was happy that Melina hadn't discussed our issues with her mother.

DING DONG! DING DONG!

I excused myself to go get the door. I didn't know if it was my mom or Dr. Bryant, but whoever it was, there presence was greatly needed. It was my mom. I allowed her entrance as she gazed at me with a worried expression on her face.

"Baby I came as quickly as I could. What's going on?" my mom asked as she hugged me close.

"Mom I fucked up," I said as she held me.

"Well, what the hell did you do son?"

DING DONG! DING DONG!

"Lemme get the door. That's Dr. Bryant," I informed my mom.

"The counselor? Your marriage counselor does house calls?"

"I told her it was an emergency."

"Oh my God! What did you do Marcus?" my mom asked.

I opened the door and let Dr. Bryant in. "Thank you so much for coming Dr. Bryant," I said as she walked in.

"Well, you said it was urgent," she responded with a nervous look on her face.

"It is. This is my mother Gail. Mom, this is Dr. Bryant," I introduced the two women.

"Nice to meet you Dr. Bryant," my mom said.

"It's a pleasure to meet you Gail," Dr. Bryant said as the two shook hands.

"Dr. Bryant, I'll show you to the family room. Mom, Melina and her mom are in the nursery with the twins. Can you please ask Melina to come join me and Dr. Bryant in the family room?" I asked.

"Okay," my mom said as she went to the nursery.

I headed to the family room with Dr. Bryant. She sat down and pulled out her pad and pen while we waited for Melina. About five minutes later, she walked into the family room and closed the door. I hated the look on my wife's face right now. She looked so heartbroken and it was all because of me.

"Hello Melina," Dr. Bryant greeted.

"You called Dr. Bryant?" Melina asked as she looked from me to the doctor with a confused look on her face.

"I did. I thought we could use her input," I admitted.

"Oh really?" Melina asked.

"Can you tell me what's going on?" Dr. Bryant asked.

"I, uh, well, I, uh..."

"His ass cheated on me!" Melina said as she pointed at me with tears in her eyes.

"Marcus is this true?" Dr. Bryant asked.

"You damn right it's true! It's so true that he made a baby too!" Melina cried.

Dr. Bryant had a shocked expression on her face but thank God she didn't gasp the way I did. I mean, I figured Melina would tell her what the deal was. I wanted to do it, but I couldn't get the words out fast enough.

"Oh boy!" Dr. Bryant finally said. "Okay, well, I can see I have my work cut out for me. But let me say this before we go any further. Melina, I know you're upset, but the fact that Marcus called me to assist the two of you shows me that he wants to save this marriage. Am I correct in that assumption Marcus?"

"Yes. I love my wife and the last thing I want is to be thrown out of my house and a divorce!" I said as I looked into Melina's eyes.

She stared for a couple of minutes before turning away. "Ugh! I can't even look at you right now," she said as her body shook with disgust.

"I'm sorry. I don't know what else to say right now, but I really am sorry."

"Sorry for what Marcus? Sorry for cheating? Sorry for making a baby behind my back? Or sorry you got caught?" Melina asked through clenched teeth.

"Sorry for everything that I'm putting you through right now," I said. "What I did was stupid and selfish, and it's a mistake I'm going to have to live with for the rest of my life."

"Well, that's a start. Before you can work through anything, an apology is necessary. Since you've already done that, we can move forward. Marcus, I see the remorse in your facial expressions. Can we talk about this affair that you had?"

"It wasn't even like that doc. There was no affair whatsoever! It was one- night... only one damn night!"

"One damn night that produced a son!" Melina cried.

"I swear doc, I didn't mean for that shit to happen. It's just that my wife and I weren't in the best place in our marriage at the time."

"So, tell me what happened? What led to you having that one- night with a stranger?" Dr. Bryant asked. "She was a stranger right? Or was she someone you knew?"

"No, I didn't know that woman until that night doc," I confessed.

"Well, tell me what happened?" Dr. Bryant coaxed.

"My wife and I had gotten in an argument the night of the Super Bowl game. She wanted me to stay home and try for a baby, but I didn't want to stay home. I mean, I didn't want to skip out on the tradition that I had with my friends. Every year, I get together with my friends at Smitty's to watch the game, so when I told Melina that I had plans already, she got really upset," I explained.

"Melina is that an accurate assessment about what transpired between the two of you that night?"

"Yea, that sounds about right."

"So, how did you feel when Marcus left you that night?" Dr. Bryant asked Melina.

"I was hurt. Not so much because he left, but mostly because of what he said to me before he left. My husband was always blaming me for the fact that I couldn't get pregnant, even though the doctor said nothing was wrong with me. When I asked him to stay home and try for a baby that night, you know what his response was doc?"

"What was his response?" Dr. Bryant asked.

"He said we could try for a baby tomorrow Melina. He said we've been trying for a baby for years and ain't shit happened." By that time, Melina was in tears again. I hated that she was feeling that way. "I was devastated. By that time, I was crying like a baby, and my husband still left me."

"I apologized for upsetting her before I left doc..."

"I didn't care about that apology after you shitted on me!" Melina said.

"So, tell me how this stranger, who I'm assuming you met at the bar, ended up pregnant with your baby," Dr. Bryant continued.

"I never expected what happened that night to happen. To be honest, I had been drinking the whole night. I won't put all the blame on the alcohol, but alcohol did play a factor in the decisions I made that night. The chick asked for a ride home, so I agreed. Once we got there, I should've dropped her off and left..."

"But you didn't! You stayed and had sex with her!" Melina said.

"Yea, and I was wrong for that. If I could take that shit back or erase that night, I would! I never meant for any of this to happen!" I said as I raised my hands in the air.

"You keep saying that shit, but it did happen Marcus! You cheated on me and had a baby with someone else! Can you understand how that makes me feel?" my wife cried.

"I do understand, but I don't know what I can do to fix it!"

"You can't fix it! The trust is broken in our marriage! Do you understand that?" Melina asked.

"Yea, I understand..."

"So, you tell me how the hell are you supposed to fix this shit without any trust?!" Melina continued to cry.

I just put my face in my hands. I didn't have any of the answers she was searching for. And no matter what I said it was the wrong thing to say.

"So, tell me what happened with the woman afterwards Marcus? How did you find out that she was pregnant?" Dr. Bryant asked.

"We ran into her at our obstetrician's office one day. We were leaving and she was coming in. I had no idea that woman was pregnant, and even when I found out, I didn't think it was mine!" I argued with conviction.

"But the baby is yours! Can you imagine what it felt like for me to find out that my husband, who didn't want to stay home and try for a baby with me, could turn around and MAKE a baby with a stranger..." She couldn't finish because she started bawling like a baby.

I stood up and went to sit next to her. I reached out to her, but she pushed me away. "Don't touch me Marcus! Please don't touch me!"

"Babe I'm sorry. I've never been sorrier about anything in my whole life," I said as tears threatened to fall from my eyes.

"Marcus can you understand why your wife is feeling the way that she feels?" Dr. Bryant asked.

"I totally get it, and I was wrong for what I did," I said. "But what else can I do besides apologize?" I was at a loss right now because I had no idea how to mend the bond that I had broken between me and my wife.

"You know what hurts the worse? When we ran into that woman at the doctor's office again a few weeks ago, she was talking about a paternity test to prove that her son belonged to my husband. I have been trying to get him to go take that test, but he kept claiming that he was too busy. Little did I know that he had taken the test already behind my back!" Melina argued.

"Marcus is that true?"

"Kalisha, the woman in question, showed up at my job with a test. I figured since she wasn't going to back down, I might as well take it and get it over with. Mind you, I still didn't think that child was mine..."

"I don't know how when HE LOOKS JUST LIKE YOU!!" Melina shouted.

"I took the test behind my wife's back because I was trying to get the woman out of our lives. That's all. I did it because I didn't want to hurt my wife anymore that I had already done," I said as I looked into Melina's eyes, hoping she would see the sincerity in my own eyes.

"I gather that the test proved you were the father, correct?"

"Correct!"

"Oh, oh, but let me tell you how I found out!" Melina jumped in. "The test along with a letter was delivered to this house by the mail carrier! Oh, and get this. The woman got our address from a check that my husband had given her... also behind my back!"

"I gave her the check to disappear!"

"Well, your little magic trick failed Copperfield!" Melina retorted.

"Instead of making things better doc, I made them worse," I confessed.

"I can see that. My question now would be where do you guys go from here? Melina, with everything that you've found out about your husband, what does that mean for your marriage?" Dr. Bryant asked.

"To be honest, I don't know what it means for this marriage! I don't know if I can get pass this!" Melina responded.

"Let me ask you something. I understand that you're hurt, and I can't say that I blame you for being hurt because you're entitled. What I need to know right now is if you still love your husband."

"I don't know how I feel about my husband right now," Melina responded.

"Yes, you do know. You guys have been through ups and downs and trials and tribulations over the past seven years. Have you ever stopped loving your husband?"

Melina looked at Dr. Bryant then at me. Then she looked back at Dr. Bryant.

"No."

"Marcus do you love your wife?"

"Very much," I responded honestly.

"Are you still interested in the woman you slept with?"

"Hell no! I tried my hardest to forget about that damn night!" I said.

"I'm going to give you guys some exercises to do until we meet for our next session. We are going back to three days a week. Seeing as how Melina just gave birth not too long ago, I can make house calls for the next eight weeks. So, we will meet every Monday, Wednesday and Friday at 5:30 in the evening if that works for the two of you," Dr. Bryant offered.

"That's fine with me," I said.

"I don't know if counseling is going to help..."

"Well, the point is to try Melina. If you aren't willing to try, that's another matter."

"Baby please don't give up on us. I love you so much, and I'm so sorry..."

"Honestly, I don't know if love is enough to hold this marriage together," Melina replied.

"Please don't say that babe," I said sadly as I looked at her.

"You betrayed me Marcus, in the worse way. Not only did you sleep with a stranger, but she had your firstborn child, a son at that. You can't possibly understand the pain that I am feeling right now," Melina said.

"Does that mean you aren't willing to try and save your marriage?" Dr. Bryant asked.

Melina took so long to answer, I thought she was going to say no.

"I'll go to counseling, but I'm not doing this for you Marcus. I'm doing it for our little girls," she stated.

"Okay, so I'll see you guys in two days." Dr. Bryant reached in her bag and pulled out a couple of sheets of paper. She handed one to each of us. "These exercises are designed to help bridge the gap between the two of you. I'm going to ask that you do them twice a day."

Melina and I looked at the papers before Melina said, "I don't think I'm ready for my husband to touch me right now, so I won't be doing these exercises."

"Melina, I know it's going to be difficult, but if you want to save your marriage, you have to do as I ask," Dr. Bryant said. "I will see the two of you soon. Please don't make any rash decisions until then."

Dr. Bryant stood up and picked up her briefcase and I walked her to the door.

"Thank you so much for coming," I said.

"You're welcome. You know Marcus, I really hope that you guys can fix this. I think the two of you make a beautiful couple," Dr. Bryant said.

"Thanks doc. I hope so too."

After Dr. Bryant had left, I returned to the family room to find that my mom and Melina's mom had joined Melina. The three of them were all standing there with their arms across their chests and man, if looks could've killed me. Now, I had to explain to these two women that I had a son with another woman.

"God give me the strength I need to get through this!" I prayed as I looked up at the ceiling.

"You had better pray," my mom said.

That was all that I could do. I needed the Lord if I had to go up against these three women.

Chapter four

Porsha

Two weeks later...

Chandler had been upset ever since his carwash was trashed. I couldn't say that I blamed him because I didn't. He had worked so hard to get his shop the way he wanted it, so for someone to ruin it that way was upsetting. Over the past couple of weeks, a crew had been working hard to get his shop up and running. Today was finally the day of his grand reopening and he was finally excited again.

He woke me up at five this morning rubbing his dick against my ass. I was in my eighth month of pregnancy, so my load was heavier now. Dr. Lambert said that the baby would start to make his way down to the birth canal soon. But just because I was uncomfortable didn't mean that I was going to refuse my man sex. He wanted it from me, and I was going to give it to him. I was well aware of that old saying, "What one won't do, another one will". I was not about to give him the ammunition he needed to go back to that bitch Maya.

As he rolled me onto my back, he kissed me softly as he petted my kitty. He removed my panties and made his way downtown. As I spread my legs open, he drove his heated tongue inside my love tunnel. The sensations coursing through my body right at this moment felt so amazing. I couldn't believe that my boo had this much skill when it came to sex.

I arched my back and humped on his tongue as he slurped and slobbered on my swollen coochie. Sex with my man these days was ten times better. He loved fucking my pussy while I was pregnant. I wondered if he'd still love it once I had the baby. He got on his knees and wiped my juices from his chin. Then he put both of my legs on his shoulders and stuffed my love bucket with his meaty pole.

"Mmmm!" I moaned as he kissed my ankle.

As he slid his tongue along my lower leg, he squeezed my breasts. As the strokes got deeper, the intensity of our lovemaking heightened, which also heightened our pleasure.

"Oh shit!" he said in a husky voice. "That pussy so good!"

"I'm about to cum!" I cried out.

"Cum on this dick baby!" Chandler commanded.

Shit, he didn't have to tell me twice. I was on the verge of having the biggest orgasm of my fucking life. I released and it felt like I pissed on myself. Chandler looked down and then at me.

"Bae you pissed on yourself?"

"What?" I asked, totally embarrassed.

"I don't know."

"What the hell?" he asked as he jumped out of the bed.

All of a sudden, I caught the most awful pain in my lower back. "Owww!" I cried.

"Aw shit! Bae you hurting?"

"Yea, a lot!" I cried.

"You probably in labor!" Chandler said nervously.

"Dammit! That means my water broke!" I said as I slid out of the bed. "Ugh! I need to take a shower!"

"You ain't got time for that!" he said.

"Chandler, I smell funny and my ass is sticky! I have to take a shower!" I said as another pain hit. "You gonna come help me or not?"

"Yea, yea, come on!"

He helped me to the bathroom and into the shower. Then he climbed in behind me and started to wash me. I was in a lot of pain, but there was no way I was going to the hospital knowing I smelled funny! When he was done washing me, he began to wash himself.

"Really bae?" I asked.

"Shit, if you was smelling funny, my dick was smelling funny!" he said with a smile.

"Owwwww!" I cried as my knees buckled from the intense pain.

"Oh shit!" Chandler cried as he rinsed off and helped me out of the shower.

After he dried me, then himself, we went into the bedroom. I threw a dress over my head, no bra and stuck my feet in my flip flops and I was ready to go. Chandler, on the other hand, had to get all dressed up with his flashy chain and Rolex watch.

"Babe can we go now, or do I need to call for an ambulance?" I asked.

These pains were constantly coming, and my patience was wearing thin. "Aight, aight. Just lemme get my J's on and we can go!" Chandler said as he went in the walk-in closet and came back out with his black and white Retros.

After he got the shoes on his feet, he grabbed the overnight bag and helped me out to the truck. Once he helped me inside, I strapped my seatbelt as another pain pushed through. As soon as Chandler jumped behind the wheel, I grabbed his arm in pain.

"Call... Dr.... Lambert," I said through panting breaths.

I handed him my phone as he put the truck in reverse. "Babe, it's a little after six. I don't think her office is open yet," he said as he handed me back the phone.

"Gotdammit!!" I cried as I held on to my belly.

"Call... Donya!!"

He took my phone again and called my cousin. "Donya, it's Chandler. I'm sorry to be calling you so early, but on my way to bring Porsha to the hospital. She asked me to call you and let you know." There was a pause before he started speaking again. "Yea, she's in a lot of pain and her water broke!" Another pause before he said, "I'll tell her. Thanks."

"What'd she say?" I asked.

"She said she's gonna get dressed and be on her way up there. She asked if I wanted her to call your mom, so I said yea."

"Okay... whoo whoo whoo, hee hee hee!" I breathed but the shit wasn't helping one bit.

We pulled into the hospital parking lot 20 minutes later. By that time, I was climbing the fucking doors and shit. Chandler rushed in and came back out with a nurse who was pushing a wheelchair. They helped me out of the truck and as the nurse rolled me in, Chandler went to park the truck. I was wheeled to the emergency room and placed on a bed. By the time Chandler came back in, the doctor had walked in.

"I understand you're in a lot of pain and your water broke," she said.

I nodded my head because I was in too much pain to speak. "Her doctor is Dr. Lambert. She wanted me to call her, but her office isn't open yet," Chandler said.

"Well, the nurse is calling her now. Let's check your cervix," the doctor said as I bent my knees. Before she could put her fingers inside me to check, she looked up at the nurse, me and Chandler with a worried expression on her face.

"What's wrong?" Chandler asked.

"Is something wrong with my baby?" I asked.

"No, we just need to rush you upstairs because you're already crowning," the emergency room doctor said.

"What? What does that mean?" Chandler asked.

"It means the baby is already in the birth canal."

She jumped on the phone and called for assistance. A couple minutes later, two other nurses rushed in and took me upstairs. As soon as I was in the room, they started an IV drip, which I hated, put the monitor on my belly, and then sat between my legs at the end of the bed. I put my feet in the stirrups and was ordered to push. A couple of pushes later, and my baby was crying his little butt off.

―"It's a boy!" the doctor said.

She cleaned the baby off then placed him on my belly. He had a head full of hair and a nose just like his daddy. His little eyes peeked open as he stared at me. The nurse came and took him over to the clear bed and did what she had to do. CJ weighed five pounds and seven ounces, which the doctor said was a good weight considering he wasn't supposed to be born for another three weeks.

"Is he healthy?" I asked nervously.

"He is," a nurse said as she smiled with us.

They continued to clean him up before bringing him over to us.

The nurse placed him on my bare chest before walking away. His little face was so small, and I smiled as he wrapped his tiny fingers around Chandler's finger. As I stared into my baby's eyes, I felt that he knew I was his mommy.

"He looks just like you," I told Chandler as I looked at him with a smile.

"He does, huh? Except for his little lips, that's all you!" He laughed as he planted a kiss on my lips and one on the top of our son's forehead.

My phone started ringing, so Chandler reached for it. "It's Donya," he said.

"She's probably in the waiting room." I looked over at the nurse and asked, "Can my cousin come in here?"

"Yea, sure. We'll be moving you to a private room in the maternity wing in a couple of hours," she said.

"Okay, thank you."

"I'ma just walk out there and see if her and your mom are here. Shit, I need to call my mom. In all the excitement, I forgot to call her," Chandler said.

He left out the room and I continued to stroke my little boy's hand. He returned a short time later with my mom and Donya. They started gushing over the baby as I laid in bed, every bit the proud mommy. Chandler was cheesing harder than any of us.

"Can I hold him?" my mom asked.

"Sure." I passed the baby to my mom.

She sat down holding CJ as we talked. Then Donya held the baby for a little while before leaving for work. She passed the baby to Chandler and he got to hold him for about 15 minutes before they came to get CJ for his first bath and shots. By the time they brought CJ back, it was time for me to be taken to the maternity wing. Once I was settled in my room, Chandler asked if it was okay if he could run by the carwash. As much as I didn't want him to leave, I knew that today was a big day for him.

"Sure babe. Just don't be too long, okay?" I asked as he kissed me and the baby.

"I'll try not to be," he said.

He kissed his mom on the cheek before walking out. My mom had left an hour ago because she had to work. Chandler's mom didn't seem to be in any rush to leave.

"Mom would you like to give CJ his bottle?" I asked.

"Oh, yes! I would love that!" she said as she grabbed one of the bottles.

She walked over to me and took the baby from my arms. He was fussing a little and I figured it was most likely because he was hungry. "I'm so tired," I said.

"Well, you go on and rest up sweetie. I'll keep watch over baby CJ," Ms. Mary said.

"Are you sure? I don't wanna be rude."

"I'm positive. You've had a big day, so I completely understand," she said with a smile.

She didn't have to say nothing else as I drifted off to LaLa Land.

Chapter five

Chandler

I couldn't believe my lil man was finally here. I was so excited to be his dad. On my way out of the hospital, I stopped by the gift shop and purchased a box of blue cigars that read, 'It's a Boy!' Then I headed to the flower shop to purchase some flowers and balloons for my baby mama. I knew that Porsha loved flowers and I wanted those delivered as soon as possible. It cost me an extra $25 to get them delivered today, but I didn't mind. On the way to the shop, I got a call from Vaughn. I was glad he called because I had forgotten to call him and let him know CJ was born.

"Wassup bro?" I answered.

"What's poppin' bro?"

"Aye man, sorry I didn't call you earlier, but I was with my ol' lady at the hospital. CJ was born this morning," I announced.

"Whaaaaat?! You finally got yo lil man, huh?" Vaughn asked. "Congrats bro!"

"Thanks man. I'm on my way to the carwash right now..."

"Oh, that's right. You got that grand opening today," he said.

"Yea, man. I'm excited all over again. It's like it's the first time I'm opening that shit up!"

"I can only imagine."

"I wouldn't have had to do that shit if them niggas hadn't fucked up my shit..."

"Yea, speaking of dem niggas, I got some news for you about the mufuggas that fucked yo shit up!" Vaughn said.

"Word! Y'all found out who did it?" I asked.

"Hell yea! When you done playing host over at the shop, swing by the trap," Vaughn said.

"Aight, you got dat!"

"Aight, I'm catch you later. And congratulations again on the wash and the baby! My bro doing big things. I'm proud of you, bro," he said.

"Thanks, brudda! I appreciate that shit!" I said with a smile. I could feel all 32 of my damn teeth trying to bust out of my mouth. "See you soon."

"Yea, aight."

I hit the end button on my steering wheel. "Damn, shit working out real nice for me. I got the wash open again. My girl just had the baby. And my bro Vaughn found out who fucked up my shit in the first place. Yea, shit shaping out real nice!!"

I was kind of upset that I had to leave Porsha though. I mean, my mom was still there when I left, but if it hadn't been for the reopening of the carwash, I could've been there right now, with her and the baby. I pulled into the carwash parking lot and parked my truck in my designated spot marked, 'Boss Man' and hopped out. I greeted customers that were outside waiting to get their cars washed. There was a line down the street, which really put a smile on my face.

I had forgotten about the cigars that I left in the truck. So, I went back in the truck and grabbed the bag of cigars. I tossed the bag in the trashcan outside and started giving out cigars. I had got the 50- count box because I knew I'd be dishing out a lot of them. People were congratulating me on the reopening of the carwash and the baby. I smiled all the way to my office. A few minutes after I sat down, there was someone at my door.

KNOCK! KNOCK!

"Come in!" I called out.

I smiled when I saw that it was Maya. I was glad to see her because I had been hoping she would come to the festivities. I stood up to greet her. I pulled her in for a warm hug. That lasted all of two seconds before she pushed herself out of my arms with a lot of discomfort written on her face.

"What's the matter? Do I stink?" I asked as I whiffed under my right and left arm.

She laughed and smirked. "Now you know darn well you don't stink! I just don't want your baby mama jumping on my back about you hugging me!"

"Ah, you ain't gotta worry about that today. Well, you ain't gotta worry about that for a while actually. She's in the hospital. My son was born this morning," I explained.

"Wow! Congratulations!" she said with a smile and another hug.

"Can I be honest with you about something?"

"Sure, what?" she asked as she stared into my eyes, my arms still around her.

"I miss this. You and I had gotten so close, like a real good friendship. Then all of a sudden, nothing. What happened to us? Like did I do something wrong?" I asked.

She pushed out of my arms and asked, "Why are you trying to rewind the present? Let's just move forward and not worry about the past."

"I'd like to do that, but I can't help but wonder what happened to us. I mean, we were friends before we took it to the next level. Then you just dropped me like a hot potato."

"I dropped you?" she asked with a questioning gaze.

"Yea, you did. No call, no text, no explanation whatsoever!"

"Maybe we should sit down for this because obviously, you've forgotten the part you played in this," she said.

I was confused as a muthafucka right now, but I sat in one of the chairs across from my desk while she sat next to me in the other one.

"What did I do?"

"You remember I asked you not to cheat on me? I told you that if you were going to be unfaithful that we didn't need to be together," Maya said with a stern look on her face.

"I remember that shit. I also remember telling you that I wouldn't cheat on you..."

"But you were dishonest when you said that."

"No, I wasn't."

"Yes, you were Chandler! And if you're going to sit here and lie to me about it, I don't wanna talk about this anymore!" she said as she started to raise herself up out of her chair.

I grabbed her by the arm and said, "Please don't leave! I'm not trying to lie to you, but I really don't know what you're talking about! You're calling me a liar like you know something, so if you do, please tell me!"

"Chandler really?"

"Yes, really? I'm confused as fuck right now! I just don't know what the hell I did to you! I never would've done anything to hurt you Maya, you gotta believe me!" I said.

I honestly had no idea why she was calling me a liar. Like what the fuck did I do?

"So, you don't recall sleeping with your baby mama while we were together?" Maya asked as she stared at me.

I had to think back and then it hit me. That night I went to Porsha's place and we slept together. But how the hell did Maya find out about that shit?

"Yea, I can see it all over your face that you remember," she said.

"I do, and I owe you an apology..."

"You don't owe me anything Chandler. If you wanted to be with her, that was fine. I just wish you would've been honest with me instead of lying," Maya said.

"How did you find out about that?" I asked, even though I had a feeling that I already knew.

"I called your phone that night, and your baby mama answered." I placed my face in my hands as Maya continued. "She was all disrespectful and stuff, but she did tell me how you had gone by to feed your baby and how the two of you were back together."

I couldn't believe Porsha had done that shit. She must have answered my phone while I was asleep. That was the only way she would've been able to get my fingerprint to unlock my phone. That shit had me real pissed right now.

"We weren't back together though. I'll admit that I slipped up when I dropped by to check on her. But we were not back together," I said sternly.

"It's okay Chandler. To be honest, I'm over it. If you wouldn't have insisted that we talk about it, I was done. I met a really nice guy and we've been seeing each other for a couple of weeks. I was upset at first because I hate when people lie to me. But that's behind us now and I hold no ill feelings towards you at all. I wish you and your baby mama nothing but happiness," she said.

"Yea, thank you. I wish the same for you."

"I can tell that you're upset, but you shouldn't be. That was months ago, and I've put it behind me. You should do the same and move forward with whatever you had planned with your baby mama, especially now that your son has been born. You should have a huge smile on your face right now. Your carwash is a success again and you're a proud father! Don't let shit from the past mess with your present and future. You hear me?!"

"Yea, I hear you."

"Well, I'll talk to you later. I just wanted to come by and congratulate you. We can meet up next week for new marketing strategies for the coming month," Maya said as she stood up.

I stood up too and smiled. "Yea, okay."

"Talk to you soon," she said as she hugged me.

"Aight."

She walked out the door and I was left with nothing but chaotic thoughts running through my mind. Why would Porsha take it upon herself to insinuate herself in my relationship like that? I couldn't believe she had done that shit. I wanted to rush back over to the hospital, but I had so much shit to do. I not only had to be here for a while longer, but I had to run by Vaughn once I left here. It was cool though because I definitely needed some distractions to get my mind off of what Porsha did.

I left the office and went to the lobby to greet customers. I tried my best to do what Maya asked and put that shit behind me, but I couldn't do it. No matter how hard I tried, I could not get our conversation off my mind. I knew Porsha wanted us to get back together, but

I didn't think she had stooped that low to get what she wanted. She never once told me what she had done.

I left the carwash around five that evening and went to the trap to speak with Vaughn. Porsha called when I was on my way there, but I was too upset to answer. Maybe if I got a couple of drinks in my system, I'd be cool to have a conversation with her, but for right now, I couldn't do it. I knew I owed it to her to be there with her while she was in the hospital, but I just couldn't fuck with her right now.

I pulled into the driveway of the trap and hopped out my truck. I did the secret knock before the door opened. I walked in and started passing out cigars to Vaughn, Sam and Bro'man.

"I didn't think you was coming bro," Vaughn said.

"Shit, I had to come. You said y'all had some info on those niggas that trashed my shit," I said.

"We got something better than info nigga," Sam said.

They led me to the back room where three niggas with pillowcases on their heads sat tied to chairs. "What the fuck yo?" I asked.

"These the niggas that fucked up yo shop bro," Vaughn said.

"Word?"

"Hell yea!" Bro'man said as he walked over and pulled off the first pillowcase.

"Shit, I don't even know this nigga!" I said as I looked at the chocolate brother with the black eye. "Nigga you know me?"

He shook his head no, which confused me. If he didn't know me, why the fuck he trashed my shop. It didn't cost me anything to get it redone because I had insurance. Suppose I didn't have insurance though. Then that $60,000 would have come from my pockets.

"So, lemme get this straight, you don't know me, but you trashed my shop."

Bro'man pulled the pillowcases off the other two dudes' heads. Jake was the first face I recognized. "Jake! You muthafucka! You did that shit?" I asked.

Now, I knew the nigga was pissed when I fired him, but I didn't think he would have taken it that far. I mean, he had mentioned the fact that he was on probation, so to me, a nigga on probation wouldn't do no shit like that. I ripped the duct tape off his mouth not giving a shit that it almost took his lips off in the process.

"Why the fuck would you do that shit?"

"Why the fuck would you fire me nigga? You knew I needed..."

WHAP!

I knew this nigga wasn't disrespecting me in my fucking hood. He must got me fucked all the way up to think that he was going to speak to me like that.

"Pass me yo piece!" I told Vaughn. I took the gun and put it to Jake's forehead and pressed the barrel hard. "Say something else smart nigga! You musta forgot who the fuck I was! Don't let the fact that I'm a business owner fool you muthafucka!"

Those other two niggas started sweating as we all waited for Jake to say something.

"Look lil niggas, it cost 60 G's to get my carwash back to the way it was. Well, truth is, it's better than it was before. But the bottom line was 60 racks. So, if one of you or all of you got 60 racks to put in my hand right now, I'ma let y'all live to see tomorrow. However, if y'all ain't got that shit... let's just say y'all niggas gon' be sleeping with the fishes tonight," I said.

"So, you gon' kill us for that shit?" Jake asked.

"Fuckin' right! You wanna know why? Cuz that was some disrespectful shit!" I responded.

"Look man, ain't none of us got no 60 G's laying around! Didn't you have insurance?"

"Don't you worry about what the fuck I had! I'm telling you 60 racks was put back in that place to fix it up. Now, you got 60 racks?" I asked Jake.

"I just told you I ain't got it!"

WHAP!

I slammed him upside the head with the 9mm.

"Oww!" he winced in bed as blood slid down the side of his face.

"I told you to watch yo fuckin' mouth nigga!" I warned as I walked to his friends. "Either one of you niggas got 60 G's for wrecking my damn shop?"

They both shook their heads furiously as tears slid from their eyes. I almost felt sorry for them muthafuckas because I knew that they didn't think they would end up here after doing what they did. But then I thought about the fact that they did fuck up my shop for no damn reason.

"So, you niggas ain't got the money it costs me to repair my shop?"

They shook their heads no. I shrugged my shoulders and looked at Bro'man and Sam before handing the gun back to Vaughn. I replaced the tape back on Jake's big mouth.

"I sure hope your moms got some nice black dresses to wear for your funerals," I said as I turned for the door.

"Kill 'em!" I ordered before I walked out.

The dudes started mumbling through the tape, but I didn't give two fucks about that shit. These niggas needed to know that I was not to be played with. Before

I bought that carwash, I was a big dope dealer and had bodied many niggas. But after getting arrested that last time, which was the second time, I couldn't afford a third strike. So, I decided to get out the game and put my money into something legit. If ever something happened to me, Chandler Jr. would be set for life. He would be his own boss and wouldn't have to worry about selling dope on the corner or no shit like that.

Vaughn walked me out and asked, "So, you headed back to the hospital meet ya girl?"

"Nah, I'm headed to the bar up the street to toss a few back. You wanna come?"

"Nah, I need to stay here and make sure ma niggas toss those bodies right. I'ma hook up witchu some other time though bro," he said as we dapped it up.

"Yea, aight. Thanks bro."

I hopped in my truck and headed to the bar, which was only a 10- minute ride away. Porsha was still ringing my phone, but I didn't want to speak to her just yet. She left a voicemail, so I listened to it.

"Babe where are you and why aren't you answering my calls? I've been waiting for you to come back for hours. Your mom left and even my girls went home, so I'm by myself with CJ. Can you please call me?

Better yet, come back over here please!" she said as she hung up. She sounded like she had been crying.

Shit, I knew her hormones were all over the place and I shouldn't be putting her through that emotional shit, but she did that. She was responsible for that shit, not me. If she had to fuck with my phone and shit, she should've said something. But no, she wanted to keep secrets and shit.

I pulled into the parking lot of the bar and walked in after securing the lock on my truck. I sat at the bar on a stool and the bartender walked over right away.

"Looks like you're having a rough night man. What can I get you?" he asked.

"Gimme a double shot of Patron," I said.

He grabbed the bottle and poured the liquor. I took the shot straight to the head. I signaled another one with my finger and he poured another double shot. Again, I took it to the head. I then asked for a glass of Remy and took it to a table. The bar had someone playing Blues music, so I listened to that and found myself mellowing out. I stayed a couple of hours then left the table. I was a little tipsy, but not tipsy enough to not be able to drive home.

Porsha was still calling me, and her name lit up the console on my way home. I still didn't feel like talking to her, so I hit the ignore button on the steering wheel. She called back three more times, then hung up. Soon after, I got a call from my mom. It was almost eight o'clock, and I didn't know why she was calling at this time, but I wasn't about to ignore that call.

"Hey ma," I answered.

"Chandler, where are you?" she asked.

"I'm on my way home. Why... wassup?"

"Have you been drinking son?"

"Nah ma, I'm straight. Wassup?"

"Chandler Williams, I know darn well you are not driving after you've been drinking!" she fussed.

"Ma, I'm fine. I'm almost home," I said.

"Why aren't you at the hospital with Porsha and CJ? That girl is over there crying her eyes out because you left earlier, and you haven't returned yet! She said she's been calling and calling, but you aren't picking up the phone. You wanna tell me why your wife..."

"She's not my wife ma..."

"Well, she's my daughter in law regardless. I just want you to explain to me why you aren't over there instead of drunk driving!"

"I'm not drunk, ma! And I ain't over there because I'm pissed with Porsha's ass right now! I don't wanna be around her because I might say some shit that I'ma regret later!" I explained.

"You're upset with the mother of your child after she just gave birth? What the hell for?" she asked.

"It's nothing for you to concern yourself with ma. We gon' work it out, I guess. But right now, I don't feel like being bothered with her," I said.

I covered my mouth and belched like a damn dinosaur. Ugh! That shit was nasty!

"I don't know what's going on with the two of you, but y'all just had a baby. So, whatever got your boxers in a bunch, you need to fix that and go back over there! Well, maybe not tonight, but first thing tomorrow. Do you understand me son?"

I hated when my mom tried to give me orders and shit, like, I wasn't a grown ass man. "Do you understand me Chandler?" she repeated.

"Yes ma'am," I said.

"Get home safe, and I will talk to you tomorrow," she said sternly.

"Yes ma'am."

"I love you, son."

"I love you too ma," I said.

We ended the call and I continued driving home with the windows down. I needed the breeze from the outside to flow throughout the truck, so I didn't fall asleep. I inhaled deeply as I threw in my Drake CD. I rapped the rest of the way home with a smile on my face.

Soon as I climbed my ass in bed, I was knocked the hell out.

Chapter six

Melina

Two weeks later...

Marcus was lucky he had called Dr. Bryant to mediate that night because if she hadn't come to our house, he would've been out on his ass. As it was now, he may not have been out of the house, but he was definitely out of my bedroom. I still hadn't gone back to work yet because I wasn't ready to put the twins in daycare. I thought about hiring a nanny but changed my mind because the last thing I needed was some young teeny bopper around my husband with his stray dick.

I had been giving him the silent treatment, not speaking about nothing but the kids, ever since I found out about Kalisha's son. I didn't know if he was visiting the little boy or not because I never asked. I didn't think that he was though because every night, he walked in the house by 5:40. He tried smiling with me and making jokes to get my attention, but I wasn't budging. As far as I was concerned, he could joke around with someone else.

However, I was horny as hell. I hadn't had sex with my husband since before the twins were born and they had just turned three months old. That had to be the longest time me and my husband hadn't had sex. Maybe tonight, I'd let him bless me with some dick. I was just torturing myself by not getting any dick or tongue from a man who was supposed to be giving it to me anytime I wanted it.

After we put the kids to bed, I brushed pass him on my way to my bedroom. He grabbed my hand and pulled me close to him. He started kissing me and rubbing my ass and that was all I needed to get my engine roaring. As we kissed our way to the master bedroom, he grazed his tongue along my neck and my pussy started clapping. I could feel my clit throbbing beneath my panties. All I wanted right now was for him to lick my tender spot.

He laid me on the bed and practically tore my panties off. I guess he needed it just as bad as I did. He threw my panties to the floor and didn't waste any time partying my folds with his fingers. He dipped his tongue inside my honey pot which caused me to moan loudly. His tongue went in and out, up and down, as I rode his face. I was in pure heaven as I released my load into his mouth.

"Oh my God!" I cried as he continued to lap up my juices.

He stood up and stared at me with a lustful look on his face. As he removed his clothes, I reached in the nightstand and pulled out the gold wrapper. He watched in surprise as I tore it open with my teeth. "What?" I asked as I rolled it onto his fattened shaft.

"We never used condoms before," he said.

"We didn't have twins before," I said.

He didn't say another word as he climbed between my legs and began to tease my opening with his big mushroom tip. "Uh uh, put it in!" I said.

I couldn't wait to feel his dick inside me. It had been way too long since I had my kitty fulfilled. He thrust into me, which caused me to yelp a little. He sucked on my neck lightly, the way I liked, as he rotated his hips against mine. "Oh shit!" I cried.

Soon after, Marcus released his own load. I wasn't mad though. I expected it and was glad that he had released this soon. If he hadn't, that would mean he had been fucking with someone else. His body shuddered on top of mine as he climaxed. His dick softened for all of two seconds. As soon as he started sucking on my breast, it popped back up. He hadn't even removed it before he started long stroking me again.

He drove his tongue into my mouth, and I kissed him hard and deep. "Turn over," he commanded. Shit, he didn't have to tell me twice.

He pulled out and I got on my hands and knees, arching my back just right. He got behind me and licked me from my clit to my anus. "Oh shit!" I crooned as my body shook with pleasure. "You so nasty!"

"Just for you baby," he whispered huskily as he continued to drive his tongue between my kitty hole and my asshole. When I couldn't take it anymore, I begged him to put his dick inside me again. He rubbed his dick against my opening, teasing me to point that I was begging him to put it in. He shoved his dick inside me from the back and I had to stuff a pillow in my mouth to keep from screaming.

"This what you wanted?" he asked as he spread my ass cheeks, driving his dick deeper inside me.

He was hitting my G-spot so good, I didn't think it would ever be the same again. He held on to my hips and pummeled deep inside me while raining kisses on the nape of my neck and shoulders. I had to admit that shit felt amazing. It had been so long. My body started shaking violently as I climaxed. Again, I had to bury my face in the pillow to keep from waking the twins.

Marcus grabbed my hair and pulled my face to his. He wrapped one hand gently around my throat as he kissed me hard while he used his other hand to play with my tender clitoris. I was so far in ecstasy that I didn't know if I'd ever find my way back to earth. Damn! That man had some good dick. I think that was the main reason I married my husband. I was attached to the dick, but over the years, I fell deeply in love with him.

I wished things between us was the way that they used to be, but they weren't. A lot had changed, but you couldn't tell by the way we were going at it right now. He released my lips and my throat and put that familiar arch in my back before banging my backside out hard.

"Oh my God!" I cried out as he hammered away.

"I love you Melina!" he said. "Tell me you love me!"

I didn't say anything, so he started pummeling deeper inside me. "Tell me you love me!" he ordered.

"I... love... you!" I screamed.

He flipped over on his back, pulling me on top of him in the reverse cowgirl position. He sat up and held my breasts from behind as I gyrated in his lap. He sucked gently on my back, causing me to go crazy as my kitty throbbed. He laid on his back as I twerked on his hardened shaft. Finally, he gripped my hips and howled like a wolf as he released a second time. My body shook as I released again.

I was exhausted by the time we were done. As I regained control of my body, I climbed off of my husband and out of the bed. "Whew!" I marveled breathlessly. I picked up my clothes off the floor as Marcus reached for a tissue to remove the soiled condom. He wiped himself off before tossing the tissue in the trashcan.

"Damn, baby! I think that was the best sex we ever had!" he said between deep breaths.

"I know right?" I said with a smile.

"Where you going?"

"To take a shower," I responded.

"You want me to join you?" he asked with a huge smile on his face.

"No, but you can close my bedroom door on your way out."

"Come again," he said with a surprised expression on his face.

"Yea, on your way to the guest room, shut my door. Oh, and check on the twins," I said.

"But I thought..."

"You thought wrong. I was horny, just like you were. We got our fix, so now you can go back to your room."

"C'mon Melina..."

"No, you c'mon Marcus! Be glad you're even still in this house!" I said.

"I am, but damn baby!"

"See you in the morning."

I was done with this conversation. I entered the bathroom and locked the door behind me. I leaned up against the door feeling completely satisfied as I inhaled and exhaled just as deeply. That man... he made me feel so good, but I wasn't about to forget the damage he had done to our marriage. No sir, he wasn't getting off that easily.

I had to do a lot of soul searching over the past couple of weeks. While I still loved my husband, it took everything I had in me to even look at him. However, I was glad that he was still here to help me with the girls. They loved their daddy and if he were to leave this house, they would miss him. But we needed to discuss what we were going to do about Kalisha's child. Just not now. The hurt he had caused to my heart was still throbbing.

Maybe once the pain subsided a little, we'd be able to discuss it further. Thank God for Dr. Bryant. She had kept her word and visited our house three days a week for the past two weeks. She said that she would give us six more home therapy sessions then we'd have to start coming to her office or have the sessions online. She said we were making progress, but I thought it was too soon to tell. I guess she was considering the fact that my husband was still breathing. If she thought that was progress, I guess I'd have to agree with her.

As I stood in the shower lathering myself up with the loofa, I felt that familiar tingle in my kitty. That was how I always felt after me and my husband made love. It was a wonderful feeling, but I had let my pussy dictate way too much of my life already. Now, it was time for my brain to do the job for me.

I rinsed myself off then stepped out of the shower. I dried my body with the soft blanket sized towel then I got dressed. I heard the twins fussing, so I went to check on them. The vision that I saw when I entered my room melted my heart. Marcus was rocking both of them in the chair while humming a lullaby to them. He smiled when he saw me, and I smiled back. He was so attentive to our daughters and that was one of the main reasons I was glad I hadn't thrown him out.

The twins were laying on either side of him on each of his shoulders, their hands locked together on his chest. A tear slipped from my eyes as I walked over to them.

"Do you want me to take one?" I asked, not really wanting to disturb them because it looked like they were going to sleep.

"You can. Only because once they fall asleep, it'll be hard for me to put them down," he said.

I reached for Marina and went to sit in the other rocking chair. As the two of us rocked our babies to sleep, I smiled. Here we were parents when we never thought we would be. We didn't just have one baby, but two. Two little girls who depended on us for everything they needed. Marcus continued humming as he stroked Karina's little back.

I held Marina close, my chin resting against her soft cheek as she nuzzled my neck. I loved the smell of my babies. I didn't mind holding them all the time, but I knew that we'd have a very hard time with them if they got too spoiled.

Fifteen minutes later, the girls were lightly snoring, so we put them in the crib with the mobile on and crept out the room. I went to the kitchen to get a drink of water because after that sexual workout, I was parched.

"Those girls are the entire reason why we have to make our marriage work," Marcus said.

"Do you think you'd still be here if I didn't know that?" I asked as I took a sip of water and leaned on the island looking at him.

"I know I fucked up Melina, but I've apologized. We're in therapy and I'm doing everything to prove to you that I love you. I made one mistake and it never happened again, and it never will. I just want my family back," he said with tears in his eyes.

"You know that if you would've been honest when that girl said y'all slept together, none of this would be happening? Of course, I would've been hurt and upset, but not to this magnitude. You do know that, right?"

"I know babe. I just didn't want to hurt your feelings, or have you looking at me the way you're looking at me right now," he said.

"Marcus, you were unfaithful in our marriage and then lied to me about it! How do you think I'm going to look at you?" I asked as I placed my hand on my hip. "I wonder if you would've ever told me about that night had she not found us."

"I wouldn't have because there would've been no reason to," he mumbled.

"We promised each other to be honest and faithful," I reminded. "And you failed on both counts. How am I supposed to trust you now?"

"Bae as God is my witness, I haven't and will never slip up like that again," he said as he raised his right hand. "I swear to God, I'll never do anything like that to hurt you again."

"You act like you deserve a prize for being faithful in our marriage..."

"I'm not saying that..."

"Good," I said as I headed to the master bedroom.

"Bae, you really not gonna let me come back to the bedroom?"

"Good night Marcus."

I went to the bedroom, closed and locked the door. I checked the baby monitor to make sure the girls were still asleep, and they were. Then I climbed in bed and buried myself beneath the covers for the rest of the night. Thank God the babies were sleeping throughout the night these days. Marcus also had a baby monitor in the spare room, which he could check just like me.

If the girls woke up, we always went to their nursery together just like when we shared a room. For that I was grateful. Marcus was a great father. It made me think about his little boy who was missing out on his father's attention and love. I shouldn't be feeling anything since he had made a baby with a stranger outside of our marriage. But I had to remind myself that the little boy did nothing wrong. He didn't ask for this life.

It was thrust upon him, so now he needed the adults in his life to behave accordingly. Dr. Bryant had spoken to Marcus about being in his son's life, but I wasn't open to him bringing the little boy over here. But I realized how wrong I was for behaving that way. While

I was in my right to feel some kind of way towards my husband, that baby boy was innocent. He didn't deserve to not have his father in his life, especially a good father like Marcus.

At some point, we'd have to have a conversation pertaining to his involvement in his son's life. He claimed he didn't want anything to do with the child because he didn't want to hurt me. He shouldn't feel that way. His time with his son shouldn't be contingent on my feelings. That was his flesh and blood, regardless of how I felt.

Chapter seven

Marcus

My wife and I had just had some of the best sex of our lives... well, at least since we've been married. I really went hard in her pussy and gave her my all... just so she could send me back to the spare bedroom. Man, I knew I had fucked up, but I needed my wife. I hated that I was the cause of us being in this situation. I knew I should've fessed up to being with Kalisha, but I was afraid that shit would be screwed up between me and my wife. Shit, just the way they were now.

I thought after that bomb sex we just had and putting the kids to be together, she would allow me back in our bedroom. Nope! She said good night and walked her sexy ass back to the master bedroom. I went to the spare bedroom and took a shower in the guest bathroom down the hall. Once I was done, I checked on the girls once more and headed to bed. I kept the baby monitor on the nightstand just in case the babies woke up.

I didn't want Melina to have to wake up by herself with them. I climbed in bed and fell sound asleep... well, after tossing and turning for about half an hour. I always had difficulty falling asleep since my wife had banished me to the guest bedroom. I was used to snuggling and cuddling with her at night. Now, I had to substitute with a pillow. And a pillow was no comparison to my wife.

One week later...

We were having a session with Dr. Bryant this evening. We had put the girls in their swing sets and played the music while it rocked them back and forth. They stared at the little mobile above them in awe.

"So, I wanted to talk to you guys about your feelings for each other now. There's also another topic I think we should speak about before I end the session. But for now, let's talk about your feelings. Melina, how are you feeling towards your husband these days?"

"Well, I love my husband Dr. Bryant. What he has done hasn't changed the way I feel about him as far as the love that I have. I just don't trust him right now."

"Marcus how do you feel about Melina?"

"Dr. Bryant, I love Melina more than anything else in this world... besides those two little girls right there. I know that I was wrong for what I did, and I wished I had told my wife the truth when she first asked. But I can't change the past. I just wanna know what I need to do so we could move forward," I said.

"We are moving forward Marcus. However, you want us to be able to take huge steps to get back to where we were before you cheated, but that's not gonna happen. This shit is gonna take some time for me to get over. Hell, I might never get over it! But I'm trying, and I deserve credit for that," Melina said.

"I'm giving you credit bae. I guess I'm looking for you to forgive and forget..."

"That's not gonna happen at the drop of a hat Marcus. I need time, and you owe me that!" my wife said.

"She's right Marcus. For the type of betrayal your wife is going through, she has every right to feel the way that she feels. Do you understand that the type of pain that is etched in her heart is going to take some time to heal?" Dr. Bryant asked.

For the next half hour, we discussed feelings and did an exercise to help bring us closer. I was all for the exercise... anything that would bring us closer together, I was ready for it.

"Now, the second thing I want to discuss with you both is the child that Marcus fathered outside of your marriage..."

"What about him?" I asked.

"I'd like to know what role you plan on playing in this little boy's life?" Dr. Bryant asked.

"With all due respect doc, I don't think that this has anything to do with our marital situation," I said.

"Quite the contrary, it has everything to do with your marriage. If you and your wife plan to move forward with this marriage, you have to discuss your plans for this child."

"I agree," my wife said.

"I don't know what I'm gonna do about the baby. Shit, I'm already in the guest room, so I'm not trying to do anything that will get me put out the whole damn house," I said.

"Marcus, this is your child and the sibling to those little girls. He is your flesh and blood just like the twins. How can you love the twins and not your firstborn and only son?" Dr. Bryant was pissing me off with these hard ass questions. "Melina if you plan to stay with Marcus and work on your marriage, I think it would be a good idea to make that child a part of your family."

"I don't know if Melina..."

"She's right."

Me and the doctor turned to look at my wife like she had done lost her mind. I thought for sure something had happened to her for her to agree to something like that. What the hell happened to the woman who was supposed to be my other half? She must be drunk or something... high on some pain meds.

"What?" I asked.

"Dr. Bryant is right. That little boy did not ask to be brought into this world. He did not ask for his dad to be a married man. Regardless of how he happened to come into this world, he didn't ask for this life. You need to be there for him just like you are for the girls," Melina said as she looked into my eyes.

"Babe I wasn't trying to cause you anymore pain."

"Marcus I'm gonna be in pain regardless. I can't let you deny your baby boy because of me."

"I'm not trying to have shit to do with that girl!" I said.

"You're going to have to deal with her for the next 18 years, at least. So, you're gonna have to find a way to deal with it," Melina said.

"Wow! You are definitely showing me a different side of you Melina," Dr. Bryant said. "I'm amazed and so proud of you."

"Thank you, but I've had a lot of time to think about this. It wasn't a decision that was easy for me to make either, but at the end of the day, I had to think about what was in the best interest of that little boy. It's either he has no dad in his life, or we deal with this together," Melina said.

I wanted to slide over to my wife and kiss her, but I knew she would push me away. "Thanks babe. I really wasn't trying to do anything that would hurt your feelings any more than I've already hurt them," I admitted.

"Trust me, this is not how I envisioned our lives when we became parents. But you owe it to that baby to be a part of his life. He is missing out on the love that you have been sharing with our girls and that's unfair to him. So, whatever you have to do to spend time with your son, do it. I'm not talking about visiting him over at HER place either!" Melina made sure I understood that she would not tolerate me visiting Cameron at Kalisha's place.

"I had no intentions on visiting him there. Hell, I had no intentions on visiting him at all," I said, being frankly honest.

"You can go get him and bring him here for visitation," Melina said.

"Wow! You never cease to amaze me!" I said. "I wanna kiss you right now..."

"We're good on that!" Melina said as she picked up her hand to stop me.

"Maybe you're good, but I'm not! I want my wife back!"

"Marcus you can't rush things. Give your wife some time. She's open to working things out, so just be patient," Dr. Bryant advised. "Well, it seems as though my time is up. I will see you guys next week, same time, same place. Marcus, you might want to make the call to your son's mother and find out when would be a good time to come get him. Don't let too much time pass before you decide to introduce yourself to him as his father. You don't want it to be a difficult transition."

"I won't. Thank you for coming," I said as the three of us stood up.

"Thank you for allowing me to come today instead of tomorrow. I had forgotten all about that family reunion this weekend. My husband and I are leaving for Virginia tomorrow at one. I wish the two of you luck with the babies this weekend," Dr. Bryant said.

"Goodbye Dr. Bryant," Melina said as she waved.

"See you next week Melina," Dr. Bryant said as I walked her out. "Give your wife some time Marcus and be patient with her."

That was easy for her to say. She got to sleep next to her husband at night. I was missing my wife something crazy, especially after the amazing sex we had last week. Once Dr. Bryant left, I heard the girls getting fussy.

"I'll make their bottles!" I said loud enough for Melina to hear in the family room.

She didn't respond, so I made the twins' bottles while thinking about the phone call I was gonna have to make to Kalisha. I wasn't sure if she was going to be open to the idea of Cameron coming over here, but it was either that or nothing. And Cameron was my son too, so if she wanted to get child support from me, she would want to make the right decision for our son.

"Son. I have a son," I said to myself.

"Yes, you do. Now, where are the bottles?" Melina asked from behind me.

When I turned to face her, she had a smirk on her face. She just sucked her teeth and turned to go back to the family room. I got the kids bottles and shook them all the way to the family room. I handed one bottle to Melina and kept the other one for the other baby.

As we sat and fed the babies, I turned to my wife and asked, "Are you sure you're okay with me bringing Cameron over here?"

She looked at me with sadness in her eyes. "I'm aware that you have another child Marcus, and I still chose to stay married to you. With that being said, it would be stupid of me to ask you to just forget about that little boy. He deserves to have you in his life just like our daughters because you are his father too. You've already missed a few months of his life. Don't miss anymore," she said.

"So, if I call Kalisha and ask if I can pick up Cameron..."

"If WE can pick up Cameron! Until I'm able to trust you, me and the girls will be going with you to pick him up and bring him back," Melina said.

"Okay. That's fine with me. I don't have anything to hide," I said.

"I hope not."

"I really don't bae. I'm serious when I said that I want our marriage back on track."

I loved and missed my wife very much. There was nothing I wanted more than for us to work this shit out. "I know. The love you have for our girls is the only reason you're still here," she said.

"What about the love that I have for you? Doesn't that count for anything?" I asked.

"Our children come first Marcus. I have to put their needs before my own."

"But I love you too Melina. I love you so much," I said.

I know you do, but at one time, you took that love for granted Marcus. I have to make sure you never do that again."

"I can promise you that I won't."

"You made that same promise to me on our wedding day, remember?"

"I know. I fucked up, but I won't do it again," I said. I hoped that she would see that I was being honest with her.

"You should call Kalisha. I'm not sure how she's gonna feel about you bringing Cameron here," Melina said.

"Well, she doesn't have much of a choice in the matter since she was so adamant about proving that I was the dad," I said.

"Call her."

"I don't have her number."

"Oh, wow! Well, lucky for you that I still have it. At least I think I do," Melina said as she pulled her phone from her back pocket.

She began scrolling through the phone until she found what she was looking for. After rattling the number off to me, I listened as the phone rang. I truly hoped Kalisha wasn't going to be an ass about this. I hadn't spoken to her since I had gone to her place that day we received those DNA results.

Chapter eight

Kalisha

I hadn't heard from Marcus for three weeks. I didn't know why I thought once he'd find out the truth about Cameron's paternity, he'd want to be a father to him. I bet it was that bitch of a wife who was keeping him from our son. I got the feeling that she wanted Marcus to be all about her kids and forget about mine. Well, if she thought I was going to just sit back and wait until hell froze over for him to be a father to my son, she had better think again.

I had just finished putting Cameron to bed when my phone started ringing. I didn't recognize the number, but I picked up anyway.

"Hello."

"Kalisha, it's Marcus."

"Wow! I thought hell was gonna freeze over before I heard from you," I said as I rolled my eyes.

"Nah, I just had some shit to work out. So, um, listen, I was wondering if I could come by and pick up Cameron tomorrow..."

"Wait, wait. Pick up Cameron tomorrow? Pick him up for what?"

My baby didn't know him. Yea, he was the daddy, but my son needed to get used to him before he took him anywhere.

"Pick him up for visitation," Marcus responded.

"Uh, I don't know if that's a good idea..."

"What? Why not?"

"Because Marcus, my baby doesn't even know you yet..."

"Our baby doesn't know me yet, but that's why I want to pick him up to spend the weekend with me. So, he can get to know me," he said.

"So, you want me to let you come pick up my son, so you can take him where for the weekend?" I asked.

"To my house! Where else would I take him?"

"I don't know. I mean, it's not like if I know you like that!"

All of a sudden, I started feeling sweaty and my anxiety level was really high. I hadn't thought about this shit at all. I thought I'd prove Marcus was my baby's daddy and that he'd come here to spend time with Cameron. I never expected him to want to come and get my baby for a weekend away from me. No, that wasn't going to happen.

"Right. You don't know me like that, but that still doesn't change the fact that Cameron is my son. I have a right to spend time with him. I thought that's what you wanted, for him to know his father!"

"It was. I mean, it is. I just thought that you would come visit him at my place..."

"Why would I do that Kalisha? I have my own house, a wife and two other children to look after. I want Cameron to meet his sisters..."

"And your wife!" I said just a little too loud.

"What does my wife have to do with this?"

"She has everything to do with this! As a matter of fact, I bet this was her idea!"

"It wasn't her idea, but she did agree to it. She wants me to spend time with my son too."

"I bet she does! If the two of you are thinking about eliminating me from my son's life..."

"What? I know you fucking lying to me!" Marcus said.

"No, I'm not lying to you. I don't know you at all Marcus, and you've been denying my baby all this time, so why should I let you see him?"

"Because I'm his father!"

"So!"

"So, let me get this straight. You wanted to prove that I was Cameron's father so bad, but now I can't spend time with him. So, why the hell did we take the damn test Kalisha?"

Damn! Talk about some shit that was coming back to bite me in the ass!

"Never mind, you don't even have to answer that question. I'ma put it to you like this, if you won't let me see my son voluntarily, I'll take you to court for visitation! And I'm sure once the judge sees all the money I done gave your ass, he or she will be more than happy to grant me visitation. Play around if you want to, but you'll see!" he said.

"Wait! So, you are seriously gonna take me to court?"

"You damn right! As soon as I hang this phone up with you, I'm gonna call my lawyer and make sure they get started on the paperwork ASAP! I promise you that by this time next week, Cameron will be visiting me and my family!" he said.

"Marcus a judge isn't gonna grant you visitation just like that!" I said. He didn't respond. "Marcus! Marcus!"

It took me a minute to realize he had hung the phone up in my face. I immediately called Donya since she was my best friend and a lawyer. I needed to find out what my rights were, or better yet, what Marcus' rights to my son were.

"Hey girl..."

"Donya, Marcus is threatening to take me to court!"

"What? Why? When?" she asked.

"He just called me asking could he come pick Cameron up tomorrow for the weekend. Of course, I told him no! I don't know him like that..."

"Uh, correct me if I'm wrong, but isn't that why you took the DNA test? To prove that he was the father because you wanted him in Cam's life?" she asked.

"Yea, but..."

"But what Kalisha? You can't have it both ways!"

"I didn't say he couldn't see Cameron. I told him that he needed to come visit him over here!" I said.

"Over here where... your place?" Donya asked.

"Yea, what's wrong with that?"

"Well, nothing except if he doesn't want to visit there, he doesn't have to."

"What? What are you saying?"

"I'm on my way over," she said.

"Okay."

Surely, Donya wasn't telling me that I had to let Marcus take my baby. I walked into the nursery to check on my son. He was sleeping peacefully while his pacifier sat in his mouth. I was going crazy waiting for Donya, so I called Porsha.

"Hello."

"Hey Porsha, what you doing?"

"Nothing. I just put my little man to sleep. What's going on?"

"Girl," I started as I blew an exasperated breath. "Everything!"

"Like what?"

"Well, for one, Marcus called tonight asking if he could take Cameron for the weekend," I said.

"Wow!"

"I know right."

"That's a good thing though, right?"

"What?"

"Isn't that why you wanted to prove he was the daddy? So he could spend time with Cameron?" she asked.

Why wasn't anyone seeing this shit from my point of view? These girls were my best friends, but they seemed to be taking Marcus' side over mine. Shit wasn't supposed to go like this at all.

"Not really. I wanted to prove that Marcus was the daddy because he kept saying he wasn't!"

"So, you did a DNA test to prove you were right?"

"Basically. I never expected him to wanna spend time with Cameron," I said in a frustrated tone.

"Okay, now I'm confused. You wanted him to accept responsibility for the baby, so you took a test..."

"NO! That's not why I took the test! You're not understanding!"

"You're right. You lost me a long time ago," she said, which frustrated me more. I felt like no one was listening to me.

"Well, maybe if you would stop chewing in my ear, you'd be able to hear better," I said.

"Well, excuse me, but CJ has been fussy all night, so this is the first chance I've had to stuff my face."

"Oh, sorry. Is he okay?"

"Yea, I gave him some Motrin and now he's sleeping."

"I'm sorry for snapping. It's just that I don't want my baby to go, but Donya says I have to..."

"So, you already spoke to Donya?" Porsha asked. "Because you know that she's a lawyer. If anyone would know, it would be her."

"Yea, I spoke to her. She's on her way over here."

"Girl, I gotta go. Chandler just walked in and he's been having a broomstick up his ass for weeks..."

"Oh wow! What's going on with y'all?"

"I wish I knew. He's been giving me the silent treatment and only speaks to me concerning CJ. I don't even know what I did. One day we were great, and the next, shit was all fucked up," she said sadly.

"Sorry to hear that. Have you asked him what's wrong?"

"Yea, but I don't think he should be mad at me for answering his phone and telling that bitch where he was..."

"Damn sis! The one thing I learned is not to answer your man's phone... ever!"

"Yea, I have regrets about answering his phone, but not about keeping my family together. No one could ever make me regret that," she said.

"Well, good luck with that," I said. "I'll talk to you soon."

"Yea, okay. I hope things work out for you."

"Me too."

We ended the call and ten minutes later, I heard a knock on my door.

I pulled the door back and let Donya in.

"What's going on girl?" she asked.

"Marcus wants visitation with Cameron!" I stressed.

"Okay," she said as she waited for me to continue.

"Okay? Is that all you have to say?"

"Yea, because I don't understand what the problem is," she said.

"Donya that man is practically a stranger to me..."

"But he's still Cam's father, honey."

"What does that mean?"

"It means that in a court of law Marcus has a right to see and spend time with his son..."

"MY SON!!" I cried as I pointed to my chest.

"Cameron is also his son sis. What did you think was going to happen when he found out that Cameron was his son? I mean, you pushed so hard to get him to acknowledge your little boy. And now that he has, you don't want him to pursue visitation?" Donya asked.

"I didn't think he'd want visitation. I mean, he wouldn't even claim Cameron as his!"

"Well, considering the two of you only had sex once, I could understand why he might be a little apprehensive to believe you were pregnant by him..."

"Whose side are you on?"

"I'm on your side, of course, but I'm also a lawyer. So, I know that the law will side with Marcus if he takes it to court."

"You have to defend me!"

"Defend you? Kalisha this is a losing battle if you take this to court," she said. "The judge will also look at the fact that he gave you $20,000."

"He gave me 10..."

"No, he gave you 20. I saw the other check that night I slept over and Cameron slept with me. For whatever reason you don't want me to know how much Marcus really gave you..."

"I wasn't really trying to keep it from you D. You're my best friend, so I don't like keeping secrets from you."

"But you still kept that from me. Not that you had to tell me because it is your business..."

"I know, but I don't want you feeling some kind of way about me. I just didn't want you to slip up and tell Joy or have my mom finding out about the money. Joy always wants to borrow from us but can never pay us back. And my mom just takes and takes from me, so at this point, I have nothing left to give her."

"If you didn't want me to tell Joy, all you had to do was say that. You didn't even ask me to keep it from her, but I haven't mentioned anything about it," Donya said. "As for your mom, I haven't seen Glenda in months." The way she was looking at me made me feel bad for lying.

"I'm sorry I lied about the money, but I really need you to fight this visitation for me!"

"Kalisha, you aren't being realistic. The courts want both parents influence in their kids' lives. The only thing that would keep them from not granting Marcus visitation would be if he were unfit. And considering how successful he is at his job, and how well he takes care of his other kids…"

"How do you know that?" I asked.

The first thing that came to mind was that my best friend was in cahoots with my baby daddy. Was Donya on Marcus' side, but lying to me about being on my side?

"You didn't see his Facebook page?" Donya asked.

"No. I didn't even know that he had a Facebook page," I said.

"Yea, he does. Look," she said as she grabbed her phone. A couple of minutes later, she showed me the phone. "He has all kind of pictures of him and the twins. He's a really good father, and Cameron would be lucky to have him in his life."

"You're supposed to be on my side, but I can't tell!"

"I am on your side, but you're not seeing things clearly. You need to take my advice and let him visit his son."

"So, I'm just supposed to let him take my child over to his house to "play- house" with his wife!" I said. I was really upset and Donya wasn't being understanding of my position.

"No, you're supposed to let your baby daddy take his son to spend time with his siblings! What is going on with you Kalisha? I mean, you were fighting to prove that Marcus was the dad..."

"Because I knew that he was!"

"Right, but now that you've proven you were right, you don't want him to have any rights! I don't get it," Donya said as she had a puzzled expression on her face.

"I didn't think he'd want any rights. He didn't even wanna be Cameron's dad!" I said.

"And now that he does, you don't want him to be. Explain that."

"I don't know how to explain it," I said.

"Do you like Marcus?" Donya asked.

"What?"

"Do you like Marcus?"

"No!"

"You do know he's married, right?" Donya asked.

"Of course, I know that. I don't want him!"

"So, what's the problem?"

"I don't know what the problem is. I just don't want him taking my son out of my house. I don't know him like that!"

"I feel that, but I'm telling you that it would be in your best interest to agree to visitation," Donya said.

"And if I don't? Will you represent me if Marcus gets a lawyer and takes me to court?"

"I'd like to say yes, honey, but you need a family court lawyer. I don't deal with family court."

"Couldn't you make an exception?" I asked.

"I'm not a family court..."

"I know, but I need your help!"

"I can refer you to a really good family court lawyer," Donya suggested. "But I really think you should reconsider. Getting a lawyer could be costly and it could wipe out all of the money that Marcus gave you. Then what?"

"Then he'll give me more," I said.

"I doubt that since you won't let him see his son," she said.

"This is crazy!".

"I know, but you need to think about what's in the best interest of your son. Won't it benefit him to have both parents in his life?"

"I guess. But I don't need him confused about who his mother is," I said.

"I doubt that Cameron won't know who his mom is. He's four months old and he sees you every day. He doesn't even know Marcus' wife. I think you're overthinking things."

"Maybe, maybe not!"

"Well, I gotta go. I have to work early in the morning," Donya said.

"Thanks for nothing D," I said, sadly coming to the realization that Marcus had the right to take my son with him.

She gave me a hug and said, "Wow! I thought I offered you some valuable advice. Let me put it to you this way since you claim that you don't know your baby daddy at all. If a man rapes a woman and that woman has a child as a product of that rape, the rapist has a right to be in that child's life."

"WHAT?!! I know you're lying!"

"Look it up sis. I would never feed you a load of bullshit."

"That's so unfair," I said.

"As unfair as it might be, it's the law. You're actually lucky that your baby daddy is a successful, loving father. It could be a lot worse," Donya advised. "I say let him pick up Cameron and see how it goes before you shut the idea down completely."

"Yea, I can see that I don't have a choice now," I said.

"You have a choice, but it won't cost you anything to make the right one." She winked at me before walking out the door.

I locked the door behind her as the tears slid from my eyes. I was frustrated because I felt like I was being forced to do something I never planned to do. I wanted to prove that Marcus was my baby daddy more than anything because he said he wasn't. I never thought that he'd be interested in getting to know Cameron, and I certainly didn't foresee him asking for my baby to spend a weekend with him and his wife.

I climbed in bed with a ton of shit on my mind, not sure how to proceed. Marcus said he was going to get a lawyer to take me to court for visitation. Donya said if I fought him on it, I'd end up broke and Marcus would win anyway. As I cried myself to sleep, all I could think about was Marcus and his wife playing parents to my baby. I climbed out of bed and went to get Cameron to come sleep with me for the night.

I just wanted to feel his little body next to me since I had to give him up tomorrow. That shit was going to be super hard to do, but I knew I had to. This shit sucks!

Chapter nine

Porsha

Things with Chandler these past few weeks had been very unhappy to say the least. He had been acting real shady ever since he found out that I was the cause of that Maya chick breaking up with him. I didn't know why the hell she felt the need to tell him about that now. I mean, she had months to tell him why she didn't want to see him anymore. Why the hell would that bitch pick the day I gave birth to tell Chandler that she and I had a conversation? That was some foul shit.

When Chandler left the hospital that day, he said he'd be back soon. Now, I knew it was the grand reopening of his carwash, but that didn't mean he had to stay gone all fucking day. He didn't come back to the hospital until three days later when I was released. He picked me up and drove me home. Apparently, he had missed CJ though. As soon as we got home, he took our baby boy out of the carrier and made him a bottle.

Then he sat in the rocking chair in the nursery and fed him the bottle. When he was done, he changed CJ and sat back in the rocker.

"Where have you been Chandler?" I asked as I stood in the doorway, arms folded over my chest.

He just looked at me but didn't respond. He turned his attention back to CJ and once the baby was asleep, he placed him in his crib. He turned the mobile on and walked out. He passed by me like I wasn't standing there. He went to the bedroom and I followed right behind him.

"Are you gonna answer me?" I asked. "You said you were coming back to the hospital three days ago, and you never returned! Why did you leave me there by myself?"

"I was here. Don't it look like the bed been slept in?"

"You had better not have been with no other bitch in this bed!"

"Really? I mean, if I did have another bitch in this bed, which I didn't, you couldn't say shit about it. This is MY house!" he said.

"OUR house!" I corrected. "I live here too!"

"Yea, you do, but show me one bill you've paid up in this muthafucka since you moved in! Show me! Just one fuckin' bill!" he said as he held up one finger. "That's what I thought. Like I said this is MY FUCKIN' HOUSE!!"

"Why are you acting this way? What the hell is wrong with you?"

"Nothing is wrong with me! I just hate bitches who disrespect me..."

"Bitches? Who you calling a bitch, Chandler?" I asked.

"Maybe I was out of line for that considering you're CJ's mom, but you disrespected me and walked around here for months like you ain't did shit!"

"What are you talking about?"

I seriously had no idea why he was treating me this way. I didn't know what I had done to him to make him trip like this. "What am I talking about? Hmm," he said as he rubbed his goatee. "How about the night you answered my phone... let's talk about that!"

I knew exactly which night he was talking about because it was the only night that I had answered his phone. "What are you talking about?"

"You know exactly what the fuck I'm talking about!" he fumed. "How dare you answer my phone and give out my personal business..."

"I don't know why the past matters so much to you! You know you didn't love that girl because if you did, you wouldn't have been asleep in my bed! What did you think you was gon' do... use me then go back to her?!"

"I used you? What the hell did I use you for Porsha?"

"My pussy! Don't act like you don't know what I'm talking about," she said.

"Girl, pussy comes a dime a dozen and for me make that two dozen! I came over here that night and we slept together, so fuckin' what! What gave you the right to answer my phone and tell Maya what the hell had just happened between us?"

"I love you Chandler! Anything I did was for our son... so he could have his mom and dad under the same roof!" I said.

"That's some bullshit and you know it!"

"It's not bullshit! All I wanted was to have a family for my son," I cried as tears started spilling. "I wasn't even thinking about that girl! I was thinking about CJ. He's the only one that matters, and in case you haven't figured it out yet, I'd do anything for my little boy!"

"You lied and you're foul for that shit!"

"Chandler you've lied to me so many times, I can't even count on one hand. At least I never cheated on you!" I said. "How is what I've done any different than all the times you disrespected me?"

"How the hell am I supposed to trust yo ass?"

"The same way I've been learning to trust you... in time!"

"I gotta get out of here," he said as he headed for the door.

"Really? I just got home and you're gonna leave me alone again?"

"I gotta go by the carwash. I got some shit to do!"

Without another word, he pushed open the door and walked out.

That was three weeks ago, and he had been treating me like bacteria ever since. His mom said I should be patient, but I was running out of patience. If he didn't change his attitude, I was going to pick up CJ and leave his ass. He had been gone all day and was just getting home. He went to the bathroom and took a shower, then came back to the kitchen and opened the fridge.

"You didn't cook?" he asked as he peered at me over his shoulder.

"No, I didn't get a chance. CJ was fussy all day. I texted you that earlier, so you could pick up something to eat," I said.

"I didn't check my messages."

"That's obvious."

He closed the fridge and grabbed his keys. "Where are you going now?" I asked.

"To get something to eat. DUH!!"

"Chandler, we need to talk."

"We can talk when I get back," he said. "If you want something from Wendy's, text me."

"What for? You don't read them."

"Starve then!" he said as he walked out the door.

I flopped down on the sofa feeling defeated. I didn't know what to do to get us back on track. We were in a really good space before he spoke to that bitch and she blabbed her big mouth. I wondered if he was pursuing her again, or if he still wanted her back. I wouldn't dare ask him because all he did these days was snap at me. I was at the end of my rope, but I loved him.

When Kalisha called, I wanted to talk to her about what was going on with me, but I couldn't. She was too engrossed with telling me what was going on with her and Marcus. I didn't see what she was complaining about though. She had a baby daddy with a great job who wanted to take care of his son and be in his life. The shit Kalisha had going on was confusing as fuck.

One minute, she wanted a daddy for her baby and the next, she didn't. She was going to have to make her mind up because it didn't sound like Marcus was playing any games. Chandler loved our son, that was never an issue. I was thankful that he helped with the baby, but the tension between us regarding his finance advisor was starting to work my nerves. If he didn't drink some 'Act Right' juice quick, fast, and in a hurry, I could see myself paying a visit to that woman sooner rather than later.

As I was about to end the call with Kalisha, Chandler walked back in. I went to the kitchen to see what he had brought me to eat. He put his food in a paper plate, threw the bag in the trash and grabbed his drink. I followed him to the living room.

"Are you serious right now? You didn't bring me anything to eat?" I asked with a hand on my hip.

He pulled his phone from his pocket and unlocked it. He turned it for me to see.

"What?" I asked as I shrugged my shoulders.

"You didn't text me that you wanted anything..."

"Woooooow!"

"I specifically told you when I left to text me what you wanted. I didn't get a text from you so no, I didn't bring shit!"

"You have some ugly ways Chandler!" I said.

"No, I don't."

"Yes, you do. You know what I like from Wendy's. You could've brought me a spicy chicken sandwich and some fries!" I argued.

"Did you text that to me?" he countered.

"You really need to ditch the attitude! I'm sick and tired of it and I don't deserve it."

"You don't deserve what?"

"For you to treat me the way that you have! I know you were upset about me answering your phone, but that was months ago! We have a son now, so can you please stop treating me like I destroyed your relationship with your one true love or something! You and that girl had just started dating, so your feelings for her couldn't have been that fucking deep!" I continued.

"You don't know how deep my feelings were..."

"They couldn't have been as deep as you were in my pussy that night!"

"Whatever Porsha!" he said as he turned the TV on.

"If something doesn't change, I'm gonna take my son and move out of here!" I warned.

"You can move if you want to, but our son ain't going nowhere! He gon' stay right here with me and my broomstick that's up my ass!" He gazed at me with an angry look on his face. I had a feeling that he might have heard me say that shit to Kalisha, but I didn't think he'd throw it in my face.

"Sorry for saying that, but..."

"Well, at least you finally apologizing for something."

"When I'm wrong, I apologize."

"Yea, cuz I don't remember you apologizing for picking up my phone that night. Nor did I hear you say sorry for answering my call."

"I ain't sorry for trying to save my family."

"There you go! This the reason we can't get past that shit, but aight..."

So, I guess that meant he was gonna go back to acting the ass.

"You don't wanna push me to far Chandler. You won't like the results."

"Is that a threat?" he asked. "You can shell out those empty threats all you want to, but I bet you don't take my son out this fuckin' house. I know that!"

"Okay. Keep thinking that you have the upper hand and shit. I'ma show you better than I can tell you," I said as I turned to go to the bedroom.

Chandler thought this was a game, but it wasn't. I was tired of this shit! I should be enjoying the fact that our son was here, but I couldn't because I was constantly worried about my relationship.

The next day, I decided it was time to face the demons that had reared its ugly head back into my life. I dressed my baby and made my way to see the bitch that had thrown a monkey wrench in my fucking relationship. I put my baby in the back seat and strapped him in. Then I climbed in the driver's seat and put the address in the navigation system.

The directions came up almost an hour away. Why did that bitch have to be on the other side of town? I made my way there and pulled into the parking lot. The sign on the door said Maya Franklin's Financial Services.

I walked in and bypassed the secretary, heading straight to the office marked, 'Maya Franklin'. "Uh excuse me," the secretary said as she followed behind me.

I busted in the office as Maya stared at me in surprise.

"I'm sorry Maya. I tried to stop her," the secretary said.

"It's okay Felicia. I'll take it from here." Once the secretary had closed the door, Maya looked at me and asked, "What are you doing here? If you're here to discuss a financial plan, you should've made an appointment..."

"Girl bye! You know darn well I'm not here to discuss nothing with you but my man."

"Your man? Girl you are way outta line!" she said.

"Am I? Me and Chandler were doing just fine until you came along..."

"I have nothing to do with you and Chandler's relationship. Just in case you didn't know, I am in a relationship and I'm very happy."

"So happy that you told Chandler about that conversation we had months ago. Huh?"

"First of all, I didn't tell Chandler that because I was trying to ruin anything y'all got going on. He asked me and kept asking me before I finally told him what happened. I wasn't trying to ruin anything that y'all had going on. So, whatever happened to your relationship was your doing, not mine. Don't put that on me!" Maya said.

"If you hadn't told him that shit, we would still be happy. We have a child, a precious little boy. But now Chandler wants to act like I don't exist! Thanks to your bony ass!"

"Let me tell you something girl. What you need to do is find you a hobby or a job or something. Obviously, you have too much time on your hands... way too much time! Now, I need you to leave my office. Your baby is only three weeks old and you out here trippin' over some man. Any man that can have you dragging that precious baby around before the doctor even released you isn't a man you should be worried about. Now, don't get me wrong, Chandler seems like a good guy. But this shit here is crazy!" she said.

"So, you're calling me crazy?"

"I'm not calling you crazy, but your situation is crazy! You seem to be working way too hard to be with a man who doesn't wanna be with you!"

I charged after her ass so fast, you would've thought she said something about my mama. "First of all bitch, you don't know shit about my relationship to comment. You need to mind your own fucking business!"

"I'll do that, right after you get your ass out of my office!" she said with an attitude. "Don't make me call the police on you!"

"Are you gonna run and tell Chandler about this visit too?"

"She don't have to," Chandler said from behind me. I was almost afraid to turn around because I knew he was going to have that 'pissed off' look on his face. "What are you doing here Porsha?"

I turned around and sure enough, he was pissed. "I could be asking you the same question," I said.

"You first. Tell me why the hell you got my three-week old son out when you should be at home with him," he said.

"I just thought it might be a good idea for me and your little "girlfriend" to have a chat. Now, what are you doing here?" I asked.

"I came to pick up some coupon books for my fuckin' customers!" he said as Maya handed him a thick packet of yellow envelopes. "Thank you, Maya. I'm sorry that my baby mama showed up at your office, especially when I know how busy you are. I can promise you that it won't happen again."

"It's cool Chandler. I'm a big girl, and I can handle your baby mama," she said.

"Is that right? I'll be back after I'm all healed up and see if you got that same energy," I said. I didn't even know why I was saying the shit that I was saying, especially in front of my baby daddy. But I was going to say anything I had to so that bitch would stay away from my man.

"She ain't gon' be back shit!" Chandler said. "Let's go!"

He made a motion for me to leave, so I did. He followed behind me and I could feel the fire from his anger steaming up the back of my neck. Once we were outside, he really let me have it.

"What were you thinking coming here?" he asked.

"I wanted to know why after so much time had passed, she would all of a sudden decide to tell you about that phone conversation."

"I pushed her to tell me why she broke up with me! Do you get that? I was the one who keep pushing for her to tell me why she left me alone!" Chandler said.

"But why? We were happy, so I don't understand why it was so important for you to know why someone else broke up with you! She should've been a non-factor by that point. Why the hell were you still holding onto that shit?"

"Because I needed to know. To be honest, that ain't your fucking business!" he said angrily. "You ain't my mom or dad. I don't owe you any fucking explanation about none of the shit I do."

"If we're together..."

"I don't know if I wanna even be with you anymore!" he admitted.

"What?"

"You heard me. All this extra shit that you doing is uncalled for and unnecessary! You had no right to bring yo ass to this girl's office... to her job! I ain't with her! She does a job for me and that's it!" he said. "I'm tired defending myself to your insecure ass!"

"What are you saying?"

"I'm saying when you heal up, maybe you need to move back to your mom's or something. You just doing too fucking much man! I'm tired of this shit," he said as he ran his hand down his face. "I'm just tired!"

With that, he turned and walked away from me, leaving me standing there dumbfounded. I didn't know what else to do, so I did the only thing I could do. I knew if anyone would have my back, it would be Chandler's mom and my cousin Donya.

I called Donya first and told her what I was thinking about doing. She told me to go for it if I felt that strongly about it. She also reminded me how much

Chandler loved me and said love would conquer all. I really wanted to believe that, but at this point, I was beginning to wonder. What was it worth to me to have my baby daddy in my life? Was it worth giving up who I was to make him happy? Only time would tell.

After I hung up with Donya, I made one more phone call. That would be a phone call that would change my life forever...

Chapter ten

Chandler

−I couldn't say that I wished I could turn back the hands of time and get Maya back because I had moved on past her. I was upset with Porsha because she had done a fucked up thing, not because I wanted Maya back. I mean, not only had Porsha answered my damn phone, but she fucked up a relationship that I had going with someone I really liked. I had true and genuine feelings for Maya... I still did. I probably would've been able to forgive Porsha for that shit a long time ago had she just said sorry. But she didn't... not one damn time.

She saw nothing wrong with what she had done. I couldn't get her to see that I wasn't mad because of my failed relationship with Maya. I was mad because she had broken the trust that I had in her. That was some deceitful shit and being a man with my background in the drug game, loyalty and honesty meant everything to me. I knew I probably sounded like a hypocrite since I had been deceitful with Porsha in the past, but she didn't hold that shit at the top of her list.

I did. I needed to know that I could trust the people who I had in my circle. I had even gone through my call list looking for Maya's number. I couldn't find any incoming calls from her for that night or after. At first, I was puzzled by it because if she had called, her information would be in my call log history. But I never found it. That could've only meant one thing... that Porsha had erased the call from the incoming call log. Yea, she had deceived me on so many levels.

That was my fault too though. I should've never slept with Porsha that night, especially after making a promise to Maya that I wouldn't cheat on her. I was sure that by spending the night with Porsha, I had sent her some mixed signals. So, I knew that I wasn't completely blameless in the situation, which was why I was trying to make our relationship work. I didn't want CJ to grow up without a father. I wanted him to know that I loved him, and I wanted to be there for him.

I just didn't know if I could be with his mother at this point. Finding her in Maya's office talking shit was the last straw. She had a baby three weeks ago and should've been home resting with our son. I didn't and couldn't understand why she had our son all over town behind her insecurities.

After I left her standing there, I headed to the carwash. Things were pretty busy as always, but I still planned to give our coupons starting tomorrow. I was running different specials just to show my customers that I appreciated them. Two hours after I got to the carwash, my mom called.

"Hey ma, what's going on with you?" I asked.

"Hey baby, I am actually on my way to your house..."

"Fa real? Why the impromptu trip? You feeling okay?"

"I feel fine. Porsha called me in tears." I rubbed the top of my head as I rolled my eyes. I should've known that she would have called my mom about that shit.

"Oh yea? I wonder what she crying about now," I said.

"Son are you really throwing her and my grandbaby out on the streets?"

"What?"

"That's what she said. I told her there had to be something she misunderstood. I didn't raise my son that way, so there ain't no way MY SON would throw his baby mama and their newborn out on the streets..."

"Ma, I did not throw neither her, nor the baby out. I don't know why she told you that or what she trying to do, but I would never throw CJ out. HE'S ONLY THREE WEEKS OLD!! You know the type of person I am, so you gotta know she's lying!"

I couldn't believe that Porsha had called my mom with that bullshit. How the fuck could she lie to my mom like that? My mom was always taking Porsha's side and I always let her, but not this time. That shit was going to stop now. I wasn't going to take the blame for some shit I didn't do.

"So, you didn't tell her that she had to leave your house?"

"Well, I kinda did, but I didn't tell her to leave this instant," I said.

"So, what exactly did you tell her son?"

"I told her that once she's healed up, I thought it might be a good idea for her to find another place to live..."

"So, you are putting her and your son out," my mom stated. By the tone of her voice, I could tell her lips were locked tightly together and she was upset.

"Not right now ma, and I ain't putting CJ out. My son is welcome to stay, but Porsha's gotta go!"

"Now you know a mother will never leave their child behind, it doesn't matter who the other person is that offered to keep them. Porsha loves CJ way too much to just pick up and leave him with you."

"Mom Porsha ain't no angel. Porsha's been doing some foul and crazy shit and I'm just tired of it. I'm sick of her interfering in my life because she got insecurities."

"Interfering with your life huh? She has insecurities huh?"

"Yea, she does..."

"And you seriously wonder why son? Look, as much as I love you, you are no saint my love. You've put Porsha through a lot of unnecessary drama on more than one occasion. Now tell me I don't know what I'm talking about," my mom said.

Dammit! Had Porsha been telling my mom all our fucking business?

"I know I did some foul shit to her..."

"Okay then."

"But that was IN THE PAST MA!! She can't keep bringing the shit I did in the past to follow us in the present and future. It ain't fair!" I said.

"Can you for one minute put yourself in her shoes? Just for a minute. She just gave birth to your son. I'm sure her self- esteem is a little low because of the weight gain toppled with her insecurities about you and these other women. She might even be suffering from postpartum," she said.

"Post what?" I asked.

"Postpartum depression. Look it up. It's a specific type of depression women get sometimes after having a baby."

"I never heard of that."

"I'm not saying that's what's going on with her, but maybe it is. I just know that from what she just told me, it doesn't sound like you're being very supportive of her son. And it doesn't sound as if she's taking it very well. She asked if she could come stay with me for a little while, so I'm driving down there to pick up her and CJ."

"Wait, what? You're picking her and CJ up and then what?"

"And then I'm gonna take them to my house," she said.

"Ma, you don't have to do that..."

"Obviously, I do. You and Porsha need some distance from one another for a little while. Maybe with some space, her absence will make your heart grow fonder and you'll remember why you fell in love with her in the first place."

"Don't count on it, ma. Porsha has been driving a wedge between us for months," I admitted. I hated getting my mom involved in my personal business, but it was pretty obvious that Porsha had no problem doing that.

"So, are you saying that you don't love her anymore?"

"I do love her ma, but this relationship ain't healthy for us. I just don't think we should continue down this road anymore, especially while we're trying to raise a baby."

"Well, I love Porsha like she's my own daughter. So, I'm gonna pray that you two can get it together for the sake of the baby. Maybe some time apart is just what y'all need."

"I don't even know why you agreed to come get her. She just had a baby. She should be at home resting," I said.

"Well, you're not home to keep an eye on her, so if she comes to my house, I'll be able to do that."

"Well, if she insists on leaving now, I'm glad she'll be with you. I'll head home to spend some time with CJ before you come get them. Be careful ma."

"I will. I want you to be nice to Porsha and it wouldn't hurt for you to spend a little time with her too. I love that girl like a daughter, so when she hurts, I hurt for her. Just the way it does when you get hurt," she said.

"I'll be nice ma."

I let Shawn know that I was leaving and headed back home. I wasn't even mad that Porsha had called my mom. I bet she did that shit for attention. She probably didn't think I'd let her leave with CJ, but she was wrong. She could go stay with my mom for as long as she wanted to, and it wouldn't bother me because I knew she would be safe. I knew my mom would keep an eye on her and she'd be alright.

I pulled into the driveway about half an hour later. I walked into the house and surprised the shit out of Porsha. "I didn't think you would be back here until later," she said.

"That was the plan, until I got a phone call from my mom. So, you were really planning to leave with my son without telling me, huh?"

"Well, I figured since you didn't want me here, you didn't want CJ..."

I raised my hand to stop her from finishing such an untrue statement. "CJ is always welcome to stay here, so don't spit out that load of garbage to me about my son!" I said as I went and scooped him up out of the swing set.

As I held him close to me, I looked at my baby mama. What the hell had gone wrong with us? At one time, Porsha and I were so in love you couldn't keep us apart. Where you would see me, you would see her. When you would see her, you would see me. Something in our relationship broke at some point, which was why

I cheated on her. I thought for the sake of our son, we could make this relationship work, but I wouldn't keep making my life miserable even for CJ's sake.

"So, it's just me you want out of here huh? Well, let me tell you something... I will never leave my son behind, not even with his daddy! You ain't about to have some other bitch playing mother to my son! We are a packaged deal! Do you understand that? That means if you don't want me, we're both outta here!"

"That's fine. My mom is on her way to pick y'all up. She feels we might need some time apart. I'm starting to think that she might be right about that. Maybe some time apart will do both of us some good."

"Time apart is what it's gonna have to be for good though. Even when I come back to Houston, I'm not going to move back in here. It's too much uncertainty about where you want this relationship to go, and as much as I love you, I can't keep putting my life on hold while I wait for you to make up your mind. So, I wish you nothing but luck for your future," she said.

"Yea, I wish the same for you. Sorry the shit didn't work out."

"No, you're not. Because at any point and time, you could've fixed things between us, but you chose not to. So, let's hope you made the best decision you could make for yourself," she said. "Don't come crawling to me later talking about how you're sorry because I won't want to hear it."

"You know an apology goes a long way. Had you apologized for answering my phone that night, shit between us probably would've been better."

"That's what this is about? You want me to apologize for breaking up your relationship with that woman?"

"NO! I wanted you to say sorry for sticking your nose in my damn business! You had no right to pick up my phone that night. You knew it wasn't nobody calling for yo ass! All you had to do was admit you made a mistake and apologize for it. But you're too fucking stubborn to do that!"

"Damn! Well, if you want an apology here... I'm sorry I answered your phone Chandler! Are you happy now? Does that make you feel better?" she asked angrily.

—"Yea, it actually does. Thank you for that."

She had finally said what I had wanted her to say all this time. I was sure that it wouldn't fix shit between us at this point, but at least she said she was sorry. So, maybe now we could move past the shit. An hour later, my mom showed up. She and I spoke briefly about how much she loved Porsha and thought she was the best woman for me. My mom was convinced that Porsha was the best thing God created since pork chops. Maybe with some time apart, I'd be able to see what she saw. For right now, time apart would do us a world of good.

I gave CJ a kiss on the forehead and inhaled his baby fresh scent before they left. I also hugged my mom and told her that I loved her. Porsha had tears in her eyes as I pulled her close to me.

"I love you so much," she said as she sniffled.

"I love you too bae, fa real," I told her, and I meant it.

Maybe I should tell her to stay and just ask my mom to spend a couple of weeks with us to help out with CJ. Maybe that would help us get our relationship back on track. But then again, maybe this time apart was what we needed.

"It'll be okay. I'll be calling you every day to check on y'all," I said.

She and my mom got in the car and backed out of the driveway. I waved goodbye to them and had just made it inside the house when I heard something that sounded like a loud boom and crunching metal. The shit was so loud, it sounded like it happened right in front of my house. As I jogged to the end of the driveway to see what had happened, I almost shitted on myself when I saw my mom's car all mangled up.

A truck had slammed into the passenger's side of my mom's car.

"WHAT THE FUCK!!" I screamed as I pulled my phone from my pocket and took off running down the street while dialing 911.

"911 what is your emergency?" asked the operator.

"My mom, baby and girl were in a car wreck! Someone hit them on the passenger side of her car!" I said. It was hard to speak clearly to the operator when I was running as fast as I was.

"Where did the accident happen sir?"

"The corner of Beechnut and 1464. COME QUICK!! OH MY GOD!! HURRY!!" I said as I made it to the vehicle and hung up. People had stopped to help as I approached the scene. "MA!! MA!!"

Of course, the baby was screaming, so I checked on him first. I was able to take his carrier out of the car. A woman walked up behind me and asked if I needed her to check my baby out. "I'm a nurse," she explained. "I'll step right over here and check him out. I promise."

I nodded my head as I handed her the infant seat. A dude ran over to me and asked, "Are these your people?

"Yea, my mom, my girl and my son!" I said as we leaned inside the car to check on my mom. "Ma! Ma you alright?" I asked.

She looked a little dazed and had some cuts on her face and neck, probably from the shattered glass. "I'm okay baby," she said weakly. She looked a little banged up, but otherwise okay. "Porsha! Porsha baby, are you alright?!" My mom called out Porsha's name but got no response.

As I looked over at her on the other side, I screamed. "PORSHA!! PORSHA!! I'M GOING TO THE OTHER SIDE MA, BUT I'M NOT LEAVING!!"

"Go check on my girl, son! Make sure she's alright," my mom said.

I rushed over to the passenger's side where several people were trying to help an unconscious and unresponsive Porsha. We couldn't even open the front or back door on the passenger's side due to the damage caused by the truck. "PORSHA!! PORSHA!! BABY IF YOU CAN HEAR ME, I NEED YOU TO OPEN YOUR EYES BABY!!" By that time, I had tears rolling down my cheeks.

I didn't know if Porsha was dead or alive, but the pain I was feeling in my heart right now hurt so badly.

I never wanted anything like this to happen to my baby mama. I knew things had been difficult for us over the past few weeks, but I never wanted some shit like this to happen.

She was unconscious with blood all over her face. She was covered in blood on her clothes and everything, so I knew it was bad. I could hear the ambulance and fire truck as they pulled up to the scene. The paramedics jumped out and rushed over.

"YOU GOTTA HELP MY GIRL!! YOU GOTTA SAVE HER!!" I cried.

"Sir, I'm gonna need you to step back and let us do our jobs!" the paramedic said.

That was when I remembered the woman that had my baby. I rushed over to the grassy area and took him from her. "Is he okay?" I asked.

"He's fine. You might want to let the EMT's check him out at the hospital, but he doesn't seem hurt," she said.

My little boy looked okay, but I knew she was right. I had to let them check him out. However, I needed them to concentrate on saving my mom and Porsha right now. I watched as they loaded my mom on a backboard and stretcher. I rushed over to her.

"How's CJ?" she asked weakly.

"He seems fine."

"Was the baby in the car too?" the EMT asked.

"Yea, but he seems fine," I said.

"We're going to need to check him out," the EMT stated.

"Okay. But I need to ride with him and get his diaper bag out the car!" I said.

They wheeled my mom in the back of the ambulance. The police came over and brought the diaper bag. "Is he going to be riding in a separate ambulance from my mom?" I asked.

"Yes. We'll take him in this ambulance."

"What about my girl?" I asked as I looked back at Porsha.

I watched as the firefighters used the jaws of life to try and get her out of the car.

"We're gonna do everything we can to save her, but I can't lie to you sir... it's bad!"

I wanted to stay behind with Porsha, but someone had to be with our son. Never in a million years did I expect something like this to happen. I climbed in the back of the ambulance with my son as the EMT placed him on a stretcher. I said a quick prayer for all three of them to survive. I had a feeling my mom and CJ would be okay, but Porsha... dammit! I couldn't help but blame myself for this shit. I hit up Donya to let her know what happened. I told her we were on our way to the hospital and she could meet us there.

"Please God, don't take my baby mama! I know it may seem like I don't care about her, but I do Lord! I love her so much! Please save her and my mom and son." By the time I finished that lil prayer, I had tears in my eyes.

The thought of losing either one of these three people would cause a void in my heart. I couldn't even think about that shit. I wanted them all to be okay, but God had the final say on who lived and who died.

It was crazy how shit happened in the blink of an eye.

Chapter eleven

Donya

When I got the call from Chandler, I didn't know why he was calling. My secretary patched the phone through, and I could tell immediately that something was wrong, just from the sound of his voice. I knew it had something to do with Porsha and wondered what the hell my cousin had did now.

"Hello," I answered when I picked up.

"Donya, it's Chandler..."

"I know Chandler. What's going on? What did my cousin do that's got you calling me?"

"There's been an accident," he said, his voice sounding sketchy.

"What kind of accident?" I asked.

"Her and my mom had just left my house when someone smashed into the passenger's side door..." From the sound of his voice, I could tell that it must have been a bad accident.

"Oh my God! Is my cousin okay? What about the baby? Is Ms. Mary alright?" I asked as I started gathering my things to leave the office early.

"My mom has a few cuts and bruises, but she seemed okay. She was talking to me when I got to the scene. CJ seems okay, but they're checking him out to be sure since he's so young..."

"Okay, what about Porsha?" I asked. He said the vehicle hit the passenger's side, so I imagined that's where my cousin was sitting since his mom was driving.

"Nah. It's not looking good yo. She's hurt pretty bad and was unconscious. You need to get to Memorial Hermann in Sugar Land," he said.

"I'm on my way!"

I ended the call and rushed out of the office. I stopped by my secretary's desk and told her, "I'm gonna be out of the office for the rest of the day and tomorrow. My cousin was in a really bad car accident."

"Oh my God! Is she gonna be alright?"

"I don't know."

"I'll keep her in my prayers," she said.

"Thank you," I said as I rushed to the elevators.

Gary was coming from down the hall when I pushed the down button. He rushed over when he saw the look on my face. "Hey, you leaving early?"

"Yea, Porsha was in a bad car accident."

"Oh, my God! Is she gonna be okay?"

"I don't know, but it's pretty bad," I said.

"Wait! Lemme go tell Sabrina I'm leaving. I'll drive you!" Gary said.

"No, that's okay..."

"Donya, you are in no condition to be driving! Just give me two minutes!" he said in a stern tone.

He was right. I shouldn't be driving. My hands were shaking, and it was taking everything in me to hold back the tears. Just thinking about losing Porsha was devastating. She was my closest relative... more like my sister than cousin.

Gary came rushing back down the hall with his briefcase. "C'mon," he said as he put his arm around me.

The elevator dinged and we got on. Gary pushed the button that would lead us to the first floor. As we walked to my car, I could see the side eyes we were getting from other people who worked in the building. I didn't care though. They were the least of my worries right now.

I handed Gary the keys to my BMW and he unlocked the doors. I slid in the smooth buttery seat and he got behind the wheel. It was kind of odd being on the passenger's side of my vehicle because I never let anyone drive my car before. While Gary drove me to the hospital, I called Kalisha, Joy, my mom and Porsha's mom. I explained to them what was going on and by the time Gary pulled into the parking lot, I was done on the phone.

We rushed inside the emergency waiting area.

"May I help you?" the woman asked.

"My cousin and her baby were in a car accident..."

"What's your cousin's name?"

"Porsha. Porsha Alexander."

She typed in Porsha's information and looked up at me. "Give me a minute to let the doctor know that her family is her."

I walked over to the waiting room and began pacing the floor. Gary sat in one of the available blue chairs staring at me sympathetically. A couple of minutes later, the double doors opened and in walked a doctor.

"I'm looking for Porsha Alexander's family," he said.

I rushed over. "How is my cousin?" I asked.

"She's in surgery..."

"Surgery?! Oh my God! What's wrong with her?"

"Well, she was hit pretty hard from the impact. Right now, she's in surgery to try and repair her lung which was punctured from one of her broken ribs. She also stopped breathing a couple of times, but we managed to bring her back. I'm worried about internal damage to her major organs other than her lung, but I won't be able to give you more specifics until we open her up. If there's a next of kin, you may want to call them."

"Oh my God, are you saying she's gonna die?!" I asked as Gary held on to me.

"I'm saying that your cousin's injuries are severe and life threatening. We are going to do everything we can to save her, but right now, I'd get the rest of your family here," the doctor said. "I'm sorry, but I have to get back to surgery. I'll come back and speak to you and your family once we're done."

He turned and walked back through the double doors, leaving me standing there with my heart in pieces. "Oh my God Gary! Porsha might not make it!" I cried as he held me close.

"Ssshh!" he shushed me as he rubbed my back. "Sometimes those doctors don't know what they're talking about. Your cousin might make it through this just fine. You just gotta pray and have faith."

I couldn't even respond as tears continued to fall from my eyes. I was sobbing so hard that my chest was hurting. "What's going on?" I heard my mom and Porsha's mom behind me.

I rushed into my mom's arms, crying on her shoulder. "What's wrong with Porsha?" my Aunt Ginny asked.

"She's in surgery," I said.

"For what?" her mom asked.

"The doctor said internal injuries, punctured lung, broken rib! He said she might not make it Aunt Ginny!" I cried.

"Oh shit! What about baby CJ?" my mom asked.

"I don't know where he is. Chandler said he seemed fine, but I haven't seen him yet."

As I finished the sentence, Chandler entered from the back through the double doors the doctor had come from. I rushed over to him to check on CJ. "Is CJ okay?" I asked.

"Yea, the doctor gave him a clean bill of health. He's hungry, so would you all mind watching him for a minute for me please. I need to go find out how my mom is feeling," he said as he looked from me to Porsha's mom. "Oh snap! You all look like y'all got some bad news. Is it Porsha? Is she gonna be alright?"

"We don't know. She's in surgery, but the doctors don't know if she'll make it," I said.

"Aw man. I can't believe that shit," Chandler said.

"I'll watch CJ for you to go check on your mom," Aunt Ginny said.

"Thank you so much. His bottle is in the bag. You just have to mix the water with the powdered milk," Chandler said.

"Okay, he'll be fine. Don't worry," Aunt Ginny said.

Chandler thanked us and then went back through the double doors. We sat down in the blue chairs as we waited for someone to deliver some news. Kalisha walked in about five minutes later, and then Joy 20 minutes later.

"Sorry I couldn't get here sooner," Joy said. "I had to wait until I had someone to cover my shift."

"Yea, I had to drop my baby off to Marcus," Kalisha said as she rolled her eyes. "Any word on Porsha?"

"It's not looking good, but she's in surgery," I said.

Gary sat next to me with his arm around my shoulder. I didn't know what I would've done if he hadn't been here. About 20 minutes later, a doctor walked in looking for us. We all rushed up to him hoping he had good news, but the look in his eyes told me otherwise. I grabbed Gary's hand for support because I could already tell what he was going to say before he opened his mouth.

"How's Porsha?" my mom asked.

"I am so sorry," the doctor said with a sad look in his eyes.

"What are you sorry for?" my aunt asked as she handed Porsha's baby to me. "What you sorry for?"

"We did everything we could ma'am, but Porsha had more internal damage than we thought," the doctor said.

"No! NO! NO!" my Aunt Ginny cried. "THIS IS A HOSPITAL!! YOU WERE SUPPOSED TO MAKE HER WELL!!"

"I'm sorry ma'am."

I held Porsha's baby close as Gary wrapped his arms around me. I couldn't believe this had happened. I had just spoken to my cousin earlier and told her that some space would do her and Chandler some good. I told her that if she went to his mom's house, he would miss her and want her back. Maybe I should've told her to stick it out or offered to let her stay with me. As long as they weren't in the same house, they were getting space.

"I wanna see my child!" my aunt said.

"Okay, sure."

"Donya you wanna come with me baby?" my aunt asked.

"Of course," I said as I handed CJ to my mom.

"I'll be waiting for you right here," Gary said.

"Thank you."

My aunt and I held hands as we followed the doctor. I could feel her hand trembling inside mine. The doctor walked us to a room marked, 'Operating Room 4'. I took a deep breath as he walked us inside.

I wasn't prepared to see Porsha that way. She had damage to her face, probably from hitting the glass before it shattered. I could tell glass had cut her face because of the marks in some spots. Not only that, but it looked like the airbag had deployed on her side. She had a huge cut from her chest to her stomach. It had been stitched closed by the doctors during surgery.

"Oh, baby, I'm so sorry this happened to you!!" Aunt Ginny said.

I didn't know what to say to her. She and Porsha hadn't been that close over the past couple of years. I imagined she was feeling some guilt from that. Tears spilled from my eyes as I stared at my cousin's lifeless body on that cold hard metal table. I couldn't imagine what she must have gone through. The doctor said that her heart had stopped a couple of times, so she probably didn't feel any pain. At least I hoped she didn't.

"We have to call the funeral home to pick up her body huh?" my aunt asked the doctor.

"Yes ma'am. But if you want, we can keep her body in the morgue while you make those arrangements," he offered.

"Yea, yea. I can't believe this is happening. A mother isn't supposed to bury her baby! I was supposed to go first!" Aunt Ginny cried.

"God makes those decisions..."

"God? Please don't talk to me about God right now doc. God failed me when he took my baby from me," my aunt said.

I knew that was her pain talking. My aunt loved God and she was always praying. She was just hurt from losing Porsha. The double doors opened, and Chandler walked in.

"NO! NO! NO!" he said as he walked closer to the table. "PORSHA BABY, YOU WEREN'T SUPPOSED TO LEAVE ME LIKE THIS!!" He was beside himself in tears and grief. I knew he had to be feeling a lot of guilt. "WHAT AM I GONNA TELL CJ?!"

He buried himself in Porsha's neck as he cried bloody murder. I knew he loved my cousin, but with the way he had been acting lately, I didn't know he still cared that much. From the way he was crying now, you would've thought she was his soulmate. The three of us were in there for about 15 minutes. By the time we left the room, I was exhausted.

I didn't even know if I had any more tears left. "How's your mom?" I asked.

"She's okay. She has a mild concussion, a few cuts and bruises, but she's okay. The doctors are gonna keep her overnight for observation."

"Are you staying with her?" I asked.

"Nah, I can't stay in this hospital with Porsha in here like that. I'ma just take CJ home. He's probably exhausted, and he shouldn't even be in this hospital anyway. He's still a newborn!" Chandler said.

"You're probably right, but are you gonna be okay by yourself?" I asked him.

"Yea, I'ma be straight. I ain't alone though. I'ma have my lil man with me."

I had my arm draped around my aunt as we walked into the waiting room. My aunt walked up to my mom and my mom took her in her arms. Kalisha was holding CJ and Gary was sitting next to her and Joy. They all stood up when we walked in. Kalisha handed the baby to Chandler and wrapped her arms around me. I heard Gary offer sympathy to Chandler. Soon after, he placed the baby in the carrier and told us goodbye before walking out.

My mom and aunt hugged me tight as we cried again. "Are you coming to the house?" my mom asked.

"No, I'm just gonna go home," I said.

"You shouldn't be by yourself baby," my mom said.

"I'm not alone mom. I have my girls and Gary's here too."

"Okay. Well, call me if you need anything," my mom said as she hugged me again.

"I'll come by the house tomorrow." My mom and aunt walked out.

Kalisha asked, "Do you want me to come spend the night with you?"

Joy said, "Yea, I can come too if you need me to, but I gotta work in the morning, so I'll be out the door by 6am."

"You don't have to sis. I'm sure you're probably tired from working all day."

"I am tired, but if you need me..."

"No, you go home boo. Thank you for coming," I said as I embraced Joy.

Kalisha stood there and smiled a sideways smile. "I can still come bestie," she said.

"Okay."

We all walked out, and they went to their cars while me and Gary walked to mine. After we were inside the car, I looked over at him. "Thank you so much for driving me."

"No problem. I can go chill with you if you need me," he offered.

"I appreciate that, but I already took up so much of your time…"

"It's not a problem. I know how close you and your cousin were."

"Yea, she was more like a sister than a first cousin," I said as tears slipped from my eyes. He handed me a tissue from inside his pocket.

"I knew these would come in handy," he said.

"And here I thought I was all out of tears."

"It's okay D. Cry as much as you need to."

He reached across the seat and held me. "I'm here for you."

"Thank you," I said as I cried against his shoulder.

He started the car and held my hand as he drove to my house. When we pulled into my driveway, Kalisha's car was already there. I forgot she said she was coming over. I guess she took my advice and let Marcus have his son for the weekend. I was glad about that because taking that shit to court would've cost her a ton of money and she would've lost.

Today seemed like a bad dream. I couldn't believe that my cousin was dead. Porsha was in the prime of her life. She had a new baby. She had a successful man. She just had so much going for her.

Why did this have to happen?

Chapter twelve

Kalisha

Getting a phone call from Donya telling me about Porsha's accident was something I was not expecting. When she asked if I could meet her at the hospital, I had to think fast about what I was going to do with my baby. I didn't want to bring him to the hospital, and I needed to be there for Donya. The only thing I could do was call Marcus and see if I could drop Cameron off. The last thing I wanted to do was bring my son over there, but my mom wasn't in town so I couldn't ask her to babysit.

I couldn't ask any of my neighbors because I didn't trust them like that.

As I waited for Marcus to answer his phone, I cringed. I didn't want to take my son there for the weekend, but what choice did I have.

"Hello."

"Marcus this is Kalisha."

"I hope you're not calling for no bullshit..."

"Actually, I need a favor."

"You just claimed to not know me last night, now you need a favor!"

"I don't have time for this! My best friend was in a car accident, so I need to go to the hospital."

"Oh my! Sorry to hear that. Is she gonna be okay?"

"I don't know. Can I please drop Cameron to your house so I can go see about my friend?" I asked.

"Yea, sure. I'm at work, so I'ma call my wife and let her know you're coming to drop the baby off," Marcus said.

Ugh! The last thing I wanted to do was drop my baby to his wife. But what choice did I have?

"Okay. Are you gonna keep him for the weekend or do I need to come get him tonight?" I asked.

"Kalisha, he's my son. I wanted to get him for the weekend," he said.

"Okay. I'll pack enough clothes for him..."

"No need. We have clothes and diapers for him at the house. Just bring his favorite blanket or stuffed animal if he has one and his milk cuz I don't know what kind of formula he's on."

"Thank you so much. I really appreciate this."

"I appreciate it too. I hope your friend is okay."

"Thank you."

We ended the call and I got my baby ready. Even though Marcus said I didn't need to bring anything, I still packed his diaper bag. I was a responsible mother, so there was no way I was going to drop my baby off without anything.

I put my baby in the car and his things, then headed to Marcus' house. Pulling into the driveway of his place made me want a house of my own. If things worked out with Marcus, I could see myself getting my own house and moving from that apartment. I got out of the car and grabbed my baby and his things.

I rang the doorbell and waited. A couple of minutes later, Marcus' wife answered the door with a smile on her face, which definitely surprised me. "Come on in," she said as she opened the door to let us in. "Oh my God! This baby is the spitting image of Marcus when he was a baby. Hold on, I'll be right back." She went to the living room and picked up a photo album. She returned with the album and turned the picture towards me. "Look."

She was right. My baby looked just like his dad when Marcus was a baby. The resemblance was scary. It was almost as if he had given birth to our child.

"You're right. It's what I had been saying all along," I said.

"You were right. Sorry about the whole paternity issue, but as a wife, I wanted to believe my husband when he said you all hadn't slept together. Now that I know the truth, we can just move on from there. I'm so sorry to hear about your friend's accident. I hope she recovers quickly."

"Thanks. Me too. Thank you for letting me bring Cameron over at the last minute."

"Of course, he's Marcus' son. I'm glad you called him instead of someone else."

Hell, what she didn't know was that I didn't have anyone else to call. If I did, Cameron and I wouldn't be here. This shit was so uncomfortable. This woman was smiling all in my face and I knew she was being fake as fuck. I couldn't even bust a smile back because she had me nervous. I was wondering when she was going to break out with the knife and stab me. That was just how nervous I was in her presence.

"You are?" I asked as I gulped hard to try and get the lump out of my throat.

"Yes. I'll tell you what I told Marcus. Regardless what we adults have going on, that has nothing to do with these kids. These kids, Cameron included, did not ask to be brought into this mess between the three of us. I want you to know that you have nothing to worry about when it comes to Cameron being here with us. Your son is in good hands," she said.

"You're a better woman than me."

"How so?"

"You just are. I guess I haven't reached that level of maturity yet," I said.

"I love my husband. I know from the two of you that y'all had a one- night stand that led to a baby being born. Sure, it caused a little friction between us, but I promise you that your baby boy won't get any static from me," Melina said. "Can I hold him?"

"Yea, sure," I said as I passed my baby to her.

"Hey lil man, hey Cameron," she said as she tickled my baby's neck. He giggled and laughed so hard that he passed gas. That was the funniest thing and the next thing I knew, the two of us were laughing right along with him.

"Well, let me get out of here. I see that my baby is in good hands," I said as I kissed Cameron on his little cheek. "You be good for your daddy and step mommy."

"I hope your friend gets better soon," Melina said.

"Thanks, me too."

I turned and walked out, headed to the hospital. I wasn't lying when I said that Melina was better than I was. Ain't no way I was about to welcome my husband's baby he made outside our fucking marriage into my damn house. On the other hand, I did appreciate her opening her house and heart to my son. If she had been some bitter bitch with an attitude, there definitely would've been a problem. I felt really good about leaving Cameron with her and Marcus.

I headed to the hospital hoping for good news, but that wasn't what I got. Damn man! I couldn't believe that Porsha was gone. She just had a baby. What was Chandler going to do without his baby mama to help him raise CJ?

Four days later...

Today was going to be one of the hardest days of our lives. Today, we were saying our final goodbyes to Porsha. At one time, Porsha and I didn't see eye to eye. But once we got pregnant and were having man problems, we became each other's support system. She had been there for me on several occasions. The same way I had been there for her. Losing her was so hard.

Cameron was still at Marcus' house. It didn't make sense to go pick him up on Sunday when I needed them to watch him today. Walking into the church, I felt like someone had punched me in the midsection. Last time I seen Porsha, she was laughing and happy. Now, looking at her in the casket, was devastating. The makeup artist at the funeral home had done a good job masking the cuts and bruises on her face and neck. If I didn't know the reality of the situation, I would've thought she was asleep.

Her mom had picked a beautiful white dress to send her home in. She looked like an angel. I said a prayer for her soul to rest easy. "Don't worry about CJ. Me, Donya and Joy will help Chandler raise him. We will make sure that he knows who his mommy was and that you loved him very much. I love you Porsha. Keep watch over us and rest easy."

As I turned around, I offered my condolences to Porsha's family, including my best friend. Chandler and his mom were sitting in the front row looking just as devastated as we all felt. I knew that Chandler's mom loved Porsha and treated her like a daughter of her own. I hated that she didn't make it. I also hated that everybody had gotten here before I did. I would've been here sooner, but it took a little longer to get my hair right. Gary and Joy were sitting with Donya, so I took my seat behind her. I touched her shoulder, so she could know that I was here for her.

The casket was closed an hour and a half later. Then the service began. The pastor walked in as the choir sang Whitney Houston's, *I Look to You*. I loved that song, but right now, it had me bawling like a baby. It had everyone crying.

As Pastor Jenkins began the opening prayer, we sat and listened. A couple of Porsha's cousins read the first two readings from the Good Book. The pastor then went back to the pulpit.

"I just wanted to talk about Porsha for a minute. I've been knowing her and her mother for years. Ms. Ginny and Porsha came to me when they were looking for a way to strengthen their relationship. Those two women are something else. For those of you who know the duo, then you how much alike they are. That's the main reason they would find it difficult to understand each other. Porsha was headstrong and stubborn, but she had a heart of gold. When I first heard the news about Porsha, the first thing I thought about was that precious little boy she gave birth to a few weeks ago. I immediately felt for Chandler, Ginny, Donya, and the rest of Porsha's family. But you all know how much Porsha loved that little boy. What we as a family and community have to do is be there for them. We have to be strong and help the family through this..."

Pastor spoke for a few more minutes, but I had zoned out. All I could think about was how me and Marcus had to make things between us work for Cameron. I felt horrible for Chandler because he now had to raise their son without his mother. Donya was right. I should consider myself lucky to have a baby daddy who cared enough about our son to want to help raise him.

Sure, getting pregnant with Cameron wasn't something we had planned for, but Marcus and his wife had stepped up to be a part of his life. I was going to be grateful for that. It could've been worse. They could've gone about their business and said fuck me and Cameron, but they didn't.

Marcus and Melina wanted to be in Cameron's life, and I was going to stop being a bitch about, like Porsha had told me to do. She said I should be happy they wanted to be a part of his life. She said I should welcome the breaks when they had him. She said I needed to let Marcus be Cameron's father since that was what I wanted. She was right. I wished that Porsha could be here to see me put my big girl panties on.

Tears for my friend came flooding from my eyes. Porsha had given me some of the best advice she could've given me. As the choir sang, *Jesus is Love* by The Commodores, there wasn't a dry eye in the church. Porsha's cousin Mike put his arm around my shoulder and held me as I cried. I was glad that he was there because I definitely needed to be held right now. My soul was so hurt because my friend wouldn't be here to laugh with us anymore.

Porsha wouldn't be here to share girl's night with us anymore. She won't be here to laugh, cry, dance, sing, or anything with us anymore. "Oh God, why did you have to take my sis?" I cried.

"It's alright Kalisha. God never makes mistakes. As hurt as we are right now, this too shall pass. We can't question God about his decision," Mike said.

He held me close and sang the song with the choir. I didn't know how he was able to do that. Don't question God. He doesn't make mistakes. This couldn't be a good thing for him to have done. Porsha being gone was hurting so many people. How could this be the right thing for her or us?

By the time it was time for us to head to the cemetery, I was so weak from all the crying. I leaned against Mike the entire time. I thanked God that he was there.

God help us get through this...

Chapter thirteen

Marcus

When I got the call from Kalisha, I just knew she was about to be on some bullshit. After talking to her last night, I had already contacted my lawyer this morning concerning visitation with my son. At first, it didn't matter whether I saw the child or not, and I knew that I was wrong for saying that. But seeing as how I didn't really know his mother, I didn't feel any type of connection to Cameron... until I held him that day.

After I took a long hard look at him, I finally saw what my wife and Kalisha had seen all along. This was my son, just as the twins were my daughters. I owed it to him to be in his life the same way I had been for my girls. I just didn't know how that was going to happen. I had already done so much to hurt my wife, so I didn't want to hurt her more than that.

But as it turned out, my wife was very mature about the situation. She didn't blame Cameron for any of this shit and encouraged me to reach out to Kalisha. What a mistake that was, or so I thought. She called me the next day and surprised the shit out of me when she asked if we could keep Cameron. Apparently, one of her friends had gotten in a car accident and she had to go to the hospital to check on her.

Of course, I agreed since I had just contacted her the night before about visitation with my son. Once I hung the phone up with her, I called Melina.

"Hello."

"Hey babe, uh, I, uh…"

"What Marcus? What did you do this time?"

"Nothing bae, I swear!"

"So, why are you calling me in the middle of the day stuttering and shit?"

"I got a call from Kalisha…"

"About what?"

"She needs to drop Cameron off because one of her friends was in a bad car accident. She needs us to watch him so she can go to the hospital," I explained.

"Oh, well, why didn't you just say that instead of all that uh, uh, uh?"

"I don't know. I guess I'm a little nervous to have you watch Cameron until I get home," I admitted.

"Nervous about what? I told you I have nothing against that baby… he is innocent Marcus!" Melina said. "I would never take out my issues on a baby."

"I know you said that, but…"

"But nothing. Is she bringing him by now?"

"Yea, she's on her way."

"Okay. I'll be waiting for her," she replied.

"Thanks bae. I really appreciate you for this," I said.

"You're welcome."

We ended the call and I got back to work. When I got home, my wife was sitting on the floor of the family room with the kids in their bouncy seats having the time of their lives. I pulled out my phone and took a picture. This was one day I'd remember for the rest of my life.

Kalisha called the next day to ask if we could keep Cameron until Monday or Tuesday.

"Hey, how's your friend?" I asked.

"She, um, she didn't make it."

"Oh my! I'm so sorry to hear that!" I said. She sounded like she had been crying all night.

"Thank you."

"Is there anything you need?" I offered.

"The funeral is Monday morning. Is it possible for me to pick Cameron up Monday evening or Tuesday please?" she asked.

"Of course. We love having him here."

"Thank you so much Marcus. I really appreciate this."

"No problem. Again, I am so sorry for your loss. Me and my wife will keep you and your friend's family in our prayers," I said.

"Thank you."

We ended the call and Melina looked at me sadly. "Her friend died?"

"Yea. I can't imagine what she's going through. It kinda makes you look at things differently huh?"

"How so?"

I pulled her close to me. "Life is too short for us to be mad with each other. I love you bae, and I promise to never do anything to hurt you again," I said.

"It has been rough getting over this betrayal, but you're right, life is too short to be holding grudges. We have three beautiful babies who are depending on the three of us to take care of them. We have to do the best we can for them."

"Does that mean you forgive me for lying?"

"I forgave you a long time ago. If I hadn't, I wouldn't have been able to open my heart to Cameron," she said.

I wrapped my arms tightly around her and held her tight. "I love you so much," I said.

"I love you too."

That was the one thing I needed to get my marriage back on track.

One month later...

Things between me and my wife had been better than ever. We had totally made up and were in the best place we could be. Me, Melina and Kalisha were able to set up a visitation schedule that worked for the three of us. We now had Cameron one week and two weekends out of the month. I also agreed to pay Kalisha $1200 a month in child support. It might seem like a lot, but when we factored in all of Cameron's expenses and her living expenses, Melina and I felt that was fair. I had my lawyer draw up the paperwork, so we could have it in writing and we all signed on the line.

That way Kalisha could never tell me that I couldn't see my son. Melina decided not to return to work, which was fine with me. I didn't want our children in daycare anyway. Plus, I made enough money, so she didn't have to work if she didn't want to. I was looking forward to getting home because my mom had agreed to keep the girls for the weekend, so me and Melina could have some quality time together.

I stopped by the flower shop on my way home and picked out an expensive bouquet of roses. Then I got back in my truck and stopped by Mikki's Soul Food Café to pick up dinner. Once I had paid for our food, I headed home with a huge smile on my face. I pulled into the garage and hopped out of the truck. I couldn't wait to get inside.

Walking into the house, I inhaled something sweet. I put the flowers on the counter and opened the oven. I smiled when I saw my wife had baked a sweet potato pie. I loved her homemade sweet potato pie. I couldn't wait to throw on a glob of whipped cream. I didn't see my wife, so I went to search for her.

"Bae! BAE! Are you home?" I asked.

As I entered the master bedroom, she was lying on the bed with a red see through negligee. Candles were lit and soft music was playing in the background. "Damn!" I said as I started removing my clothes.

"You like?" she asked with a flirtatious smile.

"Hell yea! You about to find out just how much too," I said as I climbed in bed with her.

I immediately covered her mouth with mine as our tongues danced passionately. My hands roamed my wife's body until I reached her soft spot. I pushed her panties to the side and toyed with her clit. She moaned through our kisses as I inserted two fingers into her moistened honeypot. A couple of minutes later, I removed her panties and negligee. Then I kissed and sucked on her breasts, making sure to give extra attention to her protruding nipples.

Then I kissed her belly and finally kissed her thighs. Her moans sounded so sexy that I couldn't wait any longer. I didn't waste any time thrusting my tongue into her opening. As I slid it up and down her sweet folds, she moaned loudly. She could moan as loud as she wanted to now. The kids were gone. Her mother was gone. We had the house to ourselves for the first time in a long time.

I sucked, slobbered and licked on her lady part until I tasted her sweet cream in my mouth. "Mmmm," she said. "Let me return the favor."

I gladly laid on my back as she held my pipe in her hands. She rubbed it gently but firm before wrapping her soft lips around it. She flicked her tongue over the mushroom head as she sucked it. She was able to take half of my dick in her mouth, sliding it in and out.

"Mmmm!" I moaned as my toes curled.

Several minutes later, she mounted my meaty stick and began to slide up and down my dick as I held on to her hips. "Oh my God!" she cried as she bounced like a cowgirl at the rodeo.

That shit felt so good. She leaned forward and I took her right breast in my mouth, gently sucking and nibbling on it. "Oh shit! I'm about to cum!" she cried.

Her body shook as her orgasm erupted. In one quick swoop, I had her on her back with her legs on my shoulders while I squeezed her breasts and hammered that pussy. My wife and I had been engaging in a lot of sex over the past month, but nothing like this. I wanted to touch the back of her throat with my dick. As she cried out and moaned, I continued to beat it up.

I held one leg on my shoulder and the other in the crook of my arm. She always loved the feel of that position. I continued to slave away until her body tensed, and she released again. Then I removed my dick and ordered her to turn over. She gladly got on her hands and knees so I could hit that sweet thang from behind. I drove my tongue into her pussy and ate it from behind as she moaned.

I felt her juices escaping again, got behind her and began rubbing the head of my dick against her opening. I rubbed it up and down until she was begging me to slide it in, which I gladly did. She hissed, sounding like a snake, as I entered and exited her sloppy love tunnel. That pussy was so wet that it started to make farting noises. That was when I knew it was good. As I held on to her hips, I slammed in and out of her with fervor.

"Oh my gawwwwwwdd!" she cried.

I continued to hit her G spot as I felt my nut building to the surface. I was giving her all I had to get us to that level of fulfillment. Twenty minutes or so later, I finally released inside her. We literally collapsed on the bed, totally drained from our lovemaking.

"Whew!" she whistled as she inhaled and exhaled deeply.

I stroked her thigh as I took in and blew out deep breaths. After a few minutes, we went into the bathroom to take a shower. We lathered and bathed each other as the double headed showerhead rained down on us. I kissed her soft lips before we exited the shower. We each grabbed one of the huge plush towels and dried ourselves off.

Then we headed to the bedroom and slipped into some comfortable clothes. "I cooked," Melina said with a smile.

"You did? I didn't know, so I picked up Mikki's," I said.

"Good. I meant to say I baked you a pie," she said. "All that good lovin' got me trippin'!"

She gave me a kiss as we headed to the kitchen. As soon as we rounded the corner and she saw the flowers, she gasped in surprise. "Oh my God babe! These are beautiful!" She walked over to the counter and stuck her nose in the center of the flowers, inhaling their fresh floral scent. Then she turned to me and kissed me again. "Thank you so much!"

"You're welcome. I wanted to get you something special to show you that I love you."

"Aw, babe!" She fell into my arms and I held her tight.

My wife and I had to work really hard to get to this point. We were still in therapy once a week and would probably continue therapy years down the road. I was happy that she had found it in her heart to forgive me. I didn't know what I'd do without her in my life. I had taken Melina for granted a while back, but I would never make that mistake again.

Without Melina, there was no Marcus. Only a shell of a man I didn't recognize. I needed Melina in my life because she kept me grounded. She was my backbone, my rib, my everything. As we sat down at the table to eat our food, I smiled.

"What are you smiling about?" she asked.

"About how far we've come. I almost lost you babe, but I'm gonna make sure that never happens again. I'm going to always be honest with you, no matter what."

"Thanks bae. That's the only way our marriage can work."

"I know. I won't ever keep another secret from you."

"You better not! I don't know if Dr. Bryant or our moms will be able to help next time," she said.

"There won't be a next time. I promise."

"That's good. I love you Marcus," she said as she stared deeply into my eyes.

"I love you too babe."

We leaned into each other and locked lips. I could've lost my family but thank God I hadn't. Melina and the kids meant everything to me. The fact that she accepted my son as ours made me love her ten times more. She could've hated Kalisha and Cameron, but she didn't. Her and Kalisha weren't best friends, but they were cordial with each other.

Melina realized that all Kalisha wanted was for me to step up and take care of Cameron. She wasn't out to have me for herself or nothing like that. We were just two parents raising our son together. We were still finding out new things about Kalisha every single day.

Last week, me and my boys along with her new man, helped Kalisha move into her new house. She used the money I gave her to move into a three- bedroom, two bath home. I was proud of her because I would've thought she would've blown the money on herself. But she actually put the money on something for her and Cameron's future. She was still in school trying to secure a solid future for her and our son. That was another reason why I was proud of her.

This situation wasn't ideal by any means, but it was our situation and we were working it out.

Chapter fourteen

Melina

This past month had been one of the best of my life. Not only had Marcus and I gotten our marriage back on track, but it was better than it ever was. Dr. Bryant often praised us for the growth in our marriage during our counseling sessions. Marcus always gave all the credit to me. He often said that if I hadn't been the mature one in the situation, we would've broken up and gotten a divorce. Even though I gave myself a lot of credit for keeping this marriage together, I had to give my husband some too. Marcus had grown a lot over the past four weeks. He had opened his heart to that beautiful little boy, and I was happy about that.

Cameron deserved to have his father in his life. Just because he was created during one hapless night between his parents didn't make him a mistake. After Kalisha learned of her friend's death, it was like she did a whole 360- degree turn. She wasn't the same person that I first met. I guess losing her friend opened her eyes to what was truly important, and that was making sure that Cameron had a secure future and happy home.

Even though Cameron was a month older than the girls, they were still young enough to bond with each other. But while the kids were away for the weekend, my husband and I were going to bond. We started in the bedroom, then ate dinner together while having deep conversations, and now we were going to cuddle and watch a movie on Netflix.

"You know how long it's been since we've had time to cuddle like this?" I said as I relaxed in my man's arms.

"Well, with three babies around, it's hard to get some free time," he said.

"You're right. The girls are getting so big. And little Cam..." I said as I placed my hands over my chest and batted my eyes. "He is going to be a playa when he grows up! Mark my words."

"Oh God! I hope not," Marcus said.

"Why not? I mean, he's his father's son."

"Oh, well, his father has found his queen, so that playa card been turned in!"

"Have I told you lately how much I love you?" I asked as I turned in his arms.

"I love you too, babe. Get up for a minute," he said as he gently pushed me off of him. He jumped up and headed toward the bedroom.

"Where are you going?!" I called out.

I thought we were having a very nice moment all cuddled up and lovey dovey. I wondered what my husband was up to. "Close your eyes," he said as he entered the room.

"What? Close my eyes? What for?"

"Well, you don't have to close them. I was going to give you this another time, but we may not get a chance to relax and express ourselves like this again for a while," he said.

"What are you up to?"

"We've been through so much over this past year, and all that it has shown me is that I made the right decision to ask you to be my wife. I love you more now than I ever did before. I thought it might be time for you to upgrade your wedding set. So," he said as he produced a small blue velvet box. "Can you please remove the rings on your left hand?"

"I kinda like this set babe. It's a show of your love before you started making those big bucks," I said.

"Yea, but I promise that you will love this one."

"Okay," I said as I reluctantly removed my wedding set.

"These rings symbolize the love I have for you and the recommitment of our vows that I am making to you now. I hope that you will receive this with all the love that I'm feeling inside. I want you to wear these rings and accept them as a sign of my love, fidelity, and commitment to you. Melina will you continue to be my wife for now and forever?"

"Of course," I said with tears in my eyes. "That was so beautiful."

"Not half as beautiful as you baby... or this."

Marcus opened the box with the little light at the top and I almost swallowed my tongue in shock. The ring looked like the one that Nene Leakes wore on her ring finger. Of course, it wasn't as big but mine was at least four carats. I couldn't believe Marcus had gotten me such a huge ring.

"Oh my God! You did not have to get me this!" I said as my mouth hung open. "I mean, you just bought me a truck."

"That was for giving me two babies at the same time. This is a token of my love," he said as he slid the ring on my finger.

I didn't know how I was going to get used to having this big ass ring on my finger, but I was going to figure it out. "Oh my God, babe! It's so beautiful!" I gushed as I stared at the ring in the light.

"Not as beautiful as you babe." He tilted my chin and pressed his lips to mine. I opened my mouth to receive his tongue.

Tears spilled from my eyes as I looked at the ring. I couldn't believe this shit. My man definitely deserved some of this good good, and I was sure about to bless him with some... right here, right now.

I aggressively removed his shirt and kissed him hard on the lips. We fell back on the soft, plush carpeting and I quickly pulled his dick from his boxers. Climbing on top, I kissed his slow and gently. "I love you," I whispered seductively as I nibbled on his earlobe.

"I love you too baby," he whispered huskily as he sucked on my breasts through the thin material of my shirt.

I removed my shirt as he removed my panties. He flipped me on my back and removed his boxers so fast, you would've thought he wasn't wearing any. As he entered me again, I wrapped my legs around his hips. I wanted him to make love to me, slow and sensual. As my husband and I consummated our marriage to establish our recommitment, I marveled in how far we had come. Thank God for Dr. Bryant and our mothers for helping us through. Without the three of them and our babies, I didn't think we would've made it this far.

I was so in love with my husband all over again. I knew that our marriage was solid... more solid than it had ever been.

Chapter fifteen

Donya

Suffering the loss of my sister was the worst thing I had ever gone through. Porsha was so special to me that at first, I didn't know how to get along without her. She and I had been the best of friends since we were little kids. I'd sleep over at her house or she'd sleep over at mine. Now, she was no longer here. If it wasn't for Joy, Kalisha, Gary and baby CJ, I would've fallen apart.

I was glad that Gary had been by my side through the hard times. I didn't know how I would've gotten through it without him. From the time I found out about Porsha's accident until the day and weeks after she was buried, Gary has been with me.

"I feel so bad about monopolizing all of your time," I told him the week after Porsha's funeral.

"You aren't monopolizing my time. I wanna be here with you," he said.

"Yea, but that can't be good for your relationship with Gwen. I don't want you guys arguing over me."

"Gwen and I broke up weeks ago."

"What? You never mentioned that."

"I never really had the chance. We've been busy with our caseloads and then when Porsha got in the accident... well, it just didn't seem like the right time."

"I'm sorry."

"Don't be. Donya have you ever had unresolved feelings for someone, but didn't know what to do with those feelings?" Gary asked.

"I don't know what you mean."

"I'm in love with you D. I've been in love with you for a long time but didn't say anything because I wasn't sure if it was something you wanted to pursue."

"What?" I asked in surprise. "You love me?"

"Been loving you."

"Wow!"

"If you don't feel the same way..."

I pressed my finger to his lips to shush him and climbed on his lap. "I love you too."

"You do?"

"Yea. I just didn't say anything because I thought you and Gwen were still seeing each other. I didn't wanna be the reason for your breakup," I admitted.

He didn't say another word. He brought his lips to mine and we did something we had been longing to do for long time. The kiss was so deep and passionate that before we realized it, we were naked and rolling on the living room *floor. It had been a while since I had sex, so making love to Gary in that moment set off fireworks.*

I really needed him, and he didn't hesitate to show up. As our bodies blended with each other's, I thanked God that we were finally able to share our true feelings with each other. Gary and I made love for the rest of the night. By the time we closed our eyes, we were spent and sweaty.

This was probably the first time I had smiled since losing Porsha... but it wouldn't be the last.

Ever since that night, me and Gary had been inseparable. It felt a little different working with him at work, but we were professionals. So, we continued as such. We kept our personal relationship to ourselves because it wasn't anyone's business. We went to work and did our jobs as the professionals we were and then went to his place or mine and loved on each other.

I didn't think I would be able to find any kind of happiness after my dear Porsha passed, but I did. Oh, the guy who slammed into Porsha that day was drunk driving. On behalf of Aunt Ginny, Chandler and CJ, I filed a lawsuit against the insurance company. The guy walked away from the accident with a few cuts and bruises but took something very precious from us. For that, the insurance company owed Porsha's family. No amount of money would ever bring my sis back, but it would help the family.

The guy was still in jail. Apparently, this was his fifth DUI charge, so I was pushing for him to remain locked up. He killed my cousin, so he didn't deserve to be released. Released for what... so he can do the same thing to someone else's family? No indeed.

If it was the last thing I did, I'd make sure he was never released!

Chapter sixteen

Chandler

Man, these last few weeks have been horrible. If someone had told me that I would've lost Porsha that day she left with my mom, I would've kept both of them home with me. If I would have gone with my first mind, my mom and Porsha would have been saved the tragic events that happened shortly after they left my place. I wanted to beat that drunk muthafucka's ass, but I was more concerned about my mom, son and Porsha.

My mom spent the night in the hospital and when she was released, I had to break the news to her about Porsha. My mom was devastated...

I picked her up from the hospital. When she was being wheeled to the elevator, she stopped the nurse. "I need to go visit my daughter in law."

"Your daughter in law is in this hospital?" the nurse asked.

"Yea."

"Okay, what room is she in?" the nurse asked.

"Chandler, baby, what room is Porsha in?" my mom asked.

I wanted to cry because inside I was tearing up. I just didn't want my mom to know about Porsha until I got her to the house. Donya was there watching CJ. She was going to help me break the news to my mom.

"Uh, we need to get home mama. I left CJ with Donya and she got somewhere to go in a few minutes. We gon' come back later to visit Porsha," I said.

"Okay."

We managed to get her downstairs and in the truck. I knew she was concerned about Porsha because she really loved that girl like her own. I hated that I had to be the one to tell her that Porsha was gone.

"Was Porsha hurt bad baby? How long she gon' be in the hospital?" my mom asked on the way home.

"Ma the doctor said you needed to be calm. He said not to worry too much because he didn't want to get your blood pressure up. Just relax until we get home. Can you do that for me please?" I asked.

"Why do I feel like you're hiding something from me?"

"Did you forget you have a concussion? The doctor said you need to rest."

"Okay. I just hope my girl is gonna be alright. She looked pretty banged up."

I didn't answer because I didn't know what to say. We pulled into the driveway and I parked my truck in the garage.

Then I went around to help my mom out of the truck. "Come on ma. Let's get you in the house."

"I can't wait to see the baby. I hope he's awake," she said.

"If he's not, we can get him up to spend some time with you," I said.

I got her settled on the sofa. Donya walked into the room and greeted my mom with a hug. "How are you feeling Ms. Mary?"

"I'm okay baby. My head just hurting a little bit, but I'ma be okay in a couple of days. Where's the baby?" my mom asked.

"I just put him down for a nap. Do you want me to get him?" Donya asked.

I shook my head no from behind my mom. "I'd like to talk to mom for a lil bit about Porsha," I said.

~"Ohhh," Donya said.

"What you wanna talk to me about baby? Is Porsha gon' be alright?" my mom asked.

I sat down on one side of her while Donya sat on the other side. "What's going on?"

"Ma, uh, the accident..."

"What about the accident baby?" she asked. "Did they find the man who hit us?"

"Oh, yea. His ass been in jail since that afternoon."

"Thank God. Was he hurt?"

"Ma, why you worried about him? He hit you! He could've killed you and..."

"I know baby, but that man was drunk. He didn't know what he was doing..."

"Ma, I hope that bastard gets locked up for the rest of his life for what he did!" I said. I didn't know how my mom could be concerned about that asshole. If it wasn't for his drunk ass, Porsha would still be here. My little boy would still have his mama.

"He's in jail Ms. Mary. Hopefully, he stays there," Donya said quietly as tears rolled down her cheeks.

"Aw baby, what's wrong?" my mom asked as she put her arm around Donya's shoulder. "Are you worried about Porsha? She's gonna be fine baby. We have to keep the faith and remember that God has the final say."

"Excuse me," Donya said as she jumped off and took off running.

"Aw, what's going on Chandler? Why is Donya so upset?" my mom asked, concern written all over her face.

"Ma, there's something I gotta tell you and I don't know how," I said as I ran my hand down my face. "What is it baby?"

Donya came back out with some tissue in her hand. "I'm sorry."

"It's okay. Ma, this is probably the hardest thing I ever had to tell you," I said as my eyes became watery.

"What is it baby? You're making me worried," she said as she took my hand.

I looked in my mom's eyes and could literally feel the pain she was going to feel when I told her about Porsha. "The accident... Porsha..."

"What's wrong with Porsha? She's gonna be alright, isn't she?" my mom asked.

Donya shook her head from side to side as she wiped the tears from her eyes. "She's gone Ms. Mary," Donya said.

"What you mean she's gone? Gone where?" my mom asked, confusion etched on her face. "Is she at another hospital?"

"Ma, Porsha's gone. She... she... she... she didn't make it," I said as tears rolled from my eyes.

"What are you talking about son?"

"The doctors couldn't save her Ms. Mary," Donya said as she started crying.

"Oh, God! My girl is gone?" my mom asked as the news finally hit her. "Oh, not my girl!" Tears started to spill from her eyes as she wailed for Porsha. Me and Donya wrapped our arms around her trying to comfort her while trying to comfort each other.

I knew my mom was going to take it hard, but the depth of her grief was as significant as if she had lost her own child. I could feel her pain because I was just as hurt by Porsha's passing. I wasn't even prepared to lose her so soon in *life. I didn't know how I was going to get over this. I didn't know how I was going to raise my son without his mom.*

Here I was, a month later, still grieving over losing my baby mama. My mom had moved in with me so she could help me with CJ, which was a blessing. I didn't know what I would do without her and Donya. Kalisha also dropped by one or twice a week to check on us. Ms. Ginny also came around pretty often. She was missing her daughter, so she wanted to spend as much time with CJ as she could.

I didn't mind because I knew CJ was going to have questions about his mommy when he got older. Maybe having all of these women around would help him miss Porsha less. I had a lot of guilt about letting Porsha go to my mom's house. If she and I had talked things out, she'd still be here.

They say you never know what you had until it's gone. That was so true in this case. I guess I took Porsha and her love for me for granted since I was willing to let her go. Now that she was gone, I'd do anything to have her back. I'd gladly let her answer my phone if it meant I could wake up to her again. I tried to keep busy at the carwash in an effort to not think about what I lost, but it didn't help as much as I hoped it would. There were still quiet times when all I did was think about Porsha.

My mom suggested I see a grief counselor, so I was thinking about it. I knew nothing would ever help me get over Porsha, but maybe talking to someone would help me cope better. In any case, I had to try. I was the only parent CJ had left, so I had to make sure that I was good for his sake.

"Porsha I'll always love you, bae," I said as I placed the floral bouquet on her grave. "Always. And I'll make sure that CJ knows how much you loved him. Watch over us bae. Until we meet again."

I kissed the tips of my fingers and pressed them against her headstone. Porsha was my soulmate and I didn't realize it until it was too late.

"Lord help me..."

Chapter Seventeen

Kalisha

This month had been a hard one, but I couldn't have gotten through it without my baby boy, my bestie and my new man Mike. Yea, the same Mike who let me to cry on his shoulder for Porsha's funeral. He helped me that day and every day after that. Involving myself in a relationship with him came out of the blue, but I was glad that we were able to bond in that way. In that moment, I needed someone, and he was there.

He helped me get through losing Porsha because he was also grieving. I never imagined that we'd still be together a month later. Things between me, Melina and Marcus were awesome. Who would've thought that I'd not only get along with my baby daddy, but with his wife too? I thought we'd have a cordial relationship for Cameron's sake, but it was way better than that.

Melina and I actually had conversations on the phone, invited each other to hang out, and sometimes I chilled at their place while the kids played. It was better than I ever would've imagined, and I have no one but Porsha to thank for that. She and Donya helped me see the way.

My present and future was looking brighter and brighter every day. Thanks to Mike, I now had a man of my own. He was everything I could've ever wanted, and if our relationship was half as wonderful as Marcus and Melina's I'd be a happy woman. Today, my man, my baby daddy, Cameron's Uncle Kendrick, Gary and Greg, I was all moved into my new spot. I figured with the money that Marcus had given me, I might as well invest in something bigger than an apartment. Even though Cameron was only six months, I put up a swing set in the backyard for him to swing.

I was still in school. I had a long way to go but I knew that I could do it because I was doing it for my baby boy to have a better life.

As me and Mike plopped down on the sectional sofa, I leaned my head against his shoulder. We had the house to ourselves this weekend. Marcus and Melina had Cameron so I could get moved in and hopefully, unpack some boxes. Mike had promised to help me, but we definitely weren't going to do that tonight.

"I hate moving," I said. "It takes so much out of me."

"I hope it didn't take too much out of you," he said with a smile.

"What are you thinking?" I asked.

"I'm thinking maybe we can soak in that big ass tub before bed," he said with a smile.

"Shit say no mo bae. I wanted to see what it do anyway."

He jumped up and pulled me to my feet. As we locked hands, he kissed me. Mike reminded me of a young Morris Chestnut. You know, when he played on *The Brothers*? Yea, that's the one. So, I was going to let my man run the bath water and pamper me with a nice massage.

Who would have thought that I would have matured the way that I had? I guess being with an older man helped. He ain't that much older than me... he was 31 and I was 25. Yea, me and Mike had a new relationship, but we've been knowing each other for years. It was very easy to just fall into a relationship with Mike. He was charming, funny, handsome and smart. He had his own car dealership and it was very successful.

Who knew where my relationship with Mike was going to go? But I hoped it went as far as it could. I missed Porsha a lot, but her untimely death brought me and my mom closer together, as well as me and Joy. Yea, Joy was a whole different person now that Porsha was gone. I thank God every day for the people in my life.

Marcus was a super baby daddy. Melina was definitely his better half and a great friend.

Donya was still my bestie. And Mike, well, y'all already knew what Mike was. He was my rock. If Porsha had never died, me and Mike probably would've never gotten together.

"Thanks Porsha. You're looking out for me even from heaven. Love you girl," I said as I looked upward.

"Bae I'm waiting on you," Mike called from the bathroom.

Let me not keep my man waiting.

The end!!

9 798639 365720